Accidenta

STAND-ALONE NOVEL

A Western Historical Adventure Book

by

E.J. West

RUBEDIA
PUBLISHING

Disclaimer & Copyright

Table of Contents

Letter from E.J. West

My writing is more than just stories—it's a reflection of who I am, of the land that raised me, and the woman who stole my heart. With each word, I pay homage to the rugged beauty of the American West, of my hometown, and the spirit of the frontier that courses through my veins.

This love has guided me throughout my life, despite the hardships I have encountered after my parents' death. As a young man trying to make it in the world, Wild Western stories have always been the mentor I needed to choose the right path.

As my beloved children grew and forged their own paths, I found myself yearning to reconnect with my first love—writing. With my Tracie's unwavering support, I dusted off my old notebooks and set pen to paper once again, weaving tales of cowboys and outlaws, love and loss, that echoed the rhythms of my own life.

As I grow older, I have been finding comfort in the simple pleasures of life. In my free time, you'll often find me out on the trails, riding through the Montana wilderness with my favorite horse, Chad. Horses have been my companions since childhood. There's something about the open range—the smell of pine trees, the sound of a mountain stream—that soothes the soul and reminds me of what's truly important in life.

Until the next trail, stay wild,

E.S. West

Chapter One

Late April 1852

Big Cedar, Missouri

Splintering wood pulled Cole from his thoughts. It cracked like a dead branch snapping under a heavy boot and had no business being inside Slade's Way. The orphanage ought to echo with worn floorboards groaning under the weight of thirty boys, the murmur of lessons in the common room, the clatter of spoons against tin bowls, and the calming timbre of Luke Slade's voice reading in the evenings. This new sound intruded on that, and Cole hated it.

Leaning against the staircase wall, Cole watched the spectacle taking place in the front room. Two men in dirty town clothes were methodically turning it upside down and frowning while doing it. A stout man with a drooping mustache, Sheriff Brody, upended a bookshelf. Volumes bound in worn leather—histories, poetry, books on animal husbandry that Luke insisted they all study—tumbled to the floor in a chaotic heap.

The younger and thinner one, the sheriff's deputy, yanked open drawers from a writing desk, scattering parchments and quills. The black smudges of their boot heels marred the polished floorboards that Cole and the other older boys had scrubbed on their knees just two mornings ago.

A bitter taste rose in Cole's throat. This had nothing to do with investigation. This was punishment.

The youngest boys, those no older than seven or eight, huddled in the far corner in a trembling flock of patched shirts and terrified expressions. Their whimpers flowed in a thin current beneath the noise of the destruction. A boy of six, with hair the color of straw, buried his face in the shoulder of his older brother, his small body shaking with silent sobs. The brother in question—who had a scar on his left forearm where a dog had once bit him—stood upright and stared at the two men as if he were an adult as well. Yet, he shook like a leaf in a storm, and beads of sweat pooled on his forehead.

Cole's chest burned, his large hands curling into fists at his sides.

He wanted to storm down the stairs, to plant his feet between those men and the boys, to meet their sanctioned violence with his own. But he remained still and clenched his jaw. The only thing he'd accomplish if he tried anything would be getting himself arrested.

Everyone knew Sheriff Brody took his marching orders from the town council—the same men Luke wouldn't share whiskey with or let near the boys.

What am I supposed to do against someone with the full strength of the law on his side?

Luke Slade stood in the center of the maelstrom.

The years had stooped his shoulders and etched deep lines around his kind eyes, but he held himself with unshakable dignity. He kept his hands clasped behind his back—which was a habit of his that popped up whenever he had to contain his emotions. His face paled. His lips thinned into a bloodless line. As he pleaded with the sheriff, Cole could hear the strain in his measured voice and the tremor he fought to keep hidden.

Day after day, Luke had held steady like a ship in a storm, but the waves were getting higher.

Cole had seen this look on Luke's face before—the one that swore he would die before he gave up. However, Luke's resolve had always come in the face of nature's fury or a boy's fever. Never because he had to wrestle men abusing their authority.

This sight, more than any other, solidified Cole's decision to leave, one that had been growing in his mind for months. Stories of trappers and traders passing through Big Cedar had planted the seed of it, hearing tales of vast country open under a sky so big it could swallow a man whole.

His own growing restlessness had watered it. Being a man in a boy's world. He'd outgrown the orphanage. His ambitions stretched beyond the fences that enclosed these grounds.

Luke had wanted him to take over one day and succeed him as the new caretaker of Slade's Way. Cole appreciated the thought, but it was a beautiful and comfortable cage. He loved Luke as the only father he had ever known. The boys as brothers. But he could not stay. He needed to find a place where his own name would gain value. Cole earned himself instead of getting it on a silver platter.

The chaos in front of him broke the camel's back.

With a quiet resolve that settled over him like a heavy blanket, Cole went up to his room and knelt in front of a small wooden chest at the foot of his bed. Luke had given it to him for his sixteenth birthday, and Cole had carved the name 'C. SLADE' into the lid. Inside lay his few possessions: two neatly folded spare shirts, a worn copy of Shakespeare's tragedies that Luke had given him, a small stone he'd found the first time Luke had taken him to the creek, and a leather pouch containing the money he had earned from mucking out stalls and chopping wood for folks in town.

Not much, but it was his.

He rolled the shirts tightly, placing them in the bottom of a sturdy canvas pack, and wrapped the book in a spare cloth to protect its cover. As his fingers brushed against the stone's smooth surface, he remembered the day he got it. Luke had sat with him by the water, explaining how the current had shaped the rocks over time, making them strong and smooth. 'Patience and persistence, Cole,' Luke had said. 'They can wear down any rough edge.'

Cole clenched his fist around the stone and closed his eyes.

He was leaving the man who had taught him everything, at the very moment that the man was under siege. Yet, the guilt tightening in his gut couldn't overcome the pull of the horizon.

Once he'd finished packing, Cole slung the heavy pack over one shoulder. He took one last look around the dormitory, at the rows of empty beds, the faint scent of soap and boyish sweat, and the fading afternoon light slanting through the single window. This room had held the entirety of his life until this moment.

He had fought, laughed, and whispered secrets in the dark here. Watched friend after friend leave with new families, their empty bunks reminding him of the temporary nature of every connection he had ever made. That fear of being left behind had been his companion all his life.

Now, I'm the one leaving.

He swung his shaggy brown hair—he really needed to root out that habit, it showed he was nervous—and straightened his shoulders. His posture was impeccable. Luke had always insisted that a gentleman carried himself with purpose even when he had none. Cole had a purpose now.

He turned and walked out of the room, reaching the top of the stairs just as Luke's voice rose.

"You ain't found a thing, Sheriff, 'cause there ain't nothin' to find," Luke said. "These're good boys, and this is a decent home."

9

"Council says this place's a powder keg waitin' to blow, Luke. I'm just here makin' sure they ain't talkin' smoke." He gestured to his deputy with a flick of his wrist. "Be done with it. We're through here."

Cole thudded down the stairs. Luke, who had been glaring at the sheriff, turned to Cole. His eyes swept from Cole's face down to the canvas pack on his shoulder and then back up again. The hard line of Luke's jaw went slack. The fight in his posture drained away, his shoulders slumping as if someone had dropped a pack mule's burden on them.

Luke took half a step forward. "Cole, what in God's name're you doin'?"

Cole reached the bottom of the stairs, stopping a few feet from him. He kept his eyes on Luke, ignoring the smirking sheriff and his crony as they filed out the door. The weight of every year he had spent under this roof and the debt of gratitude he could never repay sank into his gut.

He swallowed. "Figure it's high time I lit out, Luke."

Hiccupping sobs from the corner where the young ones huddled twisted Cole's gut into a knot, and he knew he deserved it. His role in the orphanage demanded he act as their big brother, looking out for them and helping them grow and achieve all their dreams, and he was leaving them.

"I can't say I like it, but I understand," Luke frowned. "You gotta do what feels right for you, son."

That word—*son*—slapped Cole. Luke used it rarely, reserving it for moments of deep pride or profound sorrow. A hot sting pricked the back of Cole's eyes, but he blinked it away, hardening his resolve. He had to do this. If he stayed now, he'd get caught in the web of guilt and obligation and might never leave. He owed Luke his life, but he couldn't give him the rest of it.

"Been mullin' over it a while. Wagons're headin' outta Kansas, and I mean to be on one." He squared his shoulders, trying to project a confidence he didn't fully feel. "Time I made my own trail, figured out what I'm worth."

Luke took another step closer. The scent of old books, pipe tobacco, and ink unique to Luke drifted between them.

"This here's your place, Cole. Ain't no one else meant to take the reins." He gestured at the overturned furniture and the scattered books. "But, you're ready to take on the world if you want to. You got the hide for it."

"You raised me tough, Luke. Showed me what's right, what's worth standin' for." A sad smile touched his lips. "Don't reckon it's a shock I'm fixin' to stand on my own now."

Luke's chin trembled, and his eyes glistened with unshed tears. He placed a hand on Cole's cheek. Calluses lined the man's palm, ones he'd have earned from a lifetime of labor in service of others.

"That trail's a thousand miles of hell—dirt, fever, arrows, and worse." Luke shook his head. "You're just a boy of eighteen."

Cole placed his hand over Luke's. "I'm a grown man, Luke. I *need* to do this."

"Yeah... I reckon you do."

"I'm grateful for everything you did for me. Every single bit of it. You raised me as your own flesh and blood, and I..." Cole's eyes watered up. "Weren't no better pa in the world I could've hoped for."

Luke pulled Cole into a fierce hug. Cole dropped his pack and wrapped his arms around the older man, burying his face for a moment in the rough wool of his coat. That familiar scent

11

of safety, home, and childhood enveloped him. The embrace bristled with unspoken words. Love and the fear of letting go. It lasted only a moment, but it *felt* like an eternity.

When Luke pulled back, he kept his hands on Cole's arms. "You keep straight out there, Cole. Be the man I know you are."

"I will."

Luke's grip tightened. "You keep your eyes sharp and your boots dry, ya hear?"

Cole nodded, unable to speak past the lump in his throat. He picked up his pack and gave Luke one last look, memorizing the face of the man who had shaped him into what he was now.

Then, he turned and walked away.

He stepped out through the doorway and into the crisp afternoon air, not daring to look back. To look back would be to break.

The dusty street of Big Cedar appeared strange to him, the familiar storefronts looking like pictures in a book he had just closed for the final time. He ignored the faces of the townsfolk who glanced at the boy with the pack leaving the troubled orphanage.

He turned west to Kansas and started walking.

Chapter Two

May 3rd, 1852

Kansas, Missouri

The journey from Big Cedar dissolved into a continuous rumble of wagon wheels and the drone of the fur trader's commentary on the quality of the pelts he was hauling. Cole— being lucky enough to hitch a ride with someone going in the same direction—had listened, nodded, and offered a hand when needed, but his mind raced ahead to the Oregon Trail.

When the trader finally pulled his team to a halt on a rise overlooking the Missouri River, a jolt shot through Cole from the soles of his boots to the roots of his hair.

The noise hit him first. The clang of a blacksmith's hammer against an anvil, the frantic braying of mules, the shouts of men haggling over prices, the rumble of countless wagon wheels, and the tinny notes of a piano spilling from the batwing doors of a saloon. The town pulsed with an untamed energy that sent a tremor down Cole's spine and pulled him forward.

He offered the fur trader a coin and his thanks and slid down from the wagon seat. As the trader's wagon creaked away, Cole stood alone at the edge of a human ocean.

For a moment, the sheer scale of it all stole the air from his lungs, shrinking him to a single speck of dust in a whirlwind. At Slade's Way, he'd been the oldest. The one Luke trusted the most and the others looked up to.

Here, he was no one.

Hollow stinging sank into his bones. He clutched his pack's leather straps, his knuckles going white, and only the gentleman's posture Luke had drilled into him kept his shoulders from slumping. He took a deep breath. Coal smoke, manure, frying bacon, and damp earth clogged the air.

A tremor ran through his hands. He wiped them on his homespun pants and forced a step forward.

***

Cole had to move with constant awareness to avoid being trampled by a freight wagon or shoved aside by a rough-looking man in a hurry. He put a hand over the small leather pouch tied to his belt, which contained the meager sum of his life's earnings. He couldn't stand around gawking.

The fur trader had given him a name: Boone Travers.

'If you want to get to Oregon and live to tell of it, you find Travers,' the man had said. 'Hard as iron, but fair. He don't run a charity, mind you, but his trains get through.'

Cole scanned the bustling encampments that fanned out from the city proper, looking for signs of a large outfit. He passed smaller groups with flimsy wagons and thin livestock. Arguments broke out over supplies, men drank from whiskey flasks in the middle of the morning, and steer wandered with empty watering troughs.

Then he saw it.

An area of disciplined activity sitting back from the main thoroughfare. A dozen wagons with clean and white canvas covers forming a semicircle. A blacksmith's forge glowed hot, the smith shaping horseshoes with rhythmic swings. Men loaded crates of flour, barrels of water, and sacks of seed into the wagon beds. The operation had a seriousness to it that stood in stark contrast to the surrounding bedlam.

At the center of it all stood a man who could only be Boone Travers.

Though of average height, he commanded the space around him as if he were a giant. He stood with his feet planted wide, his hands on his hips, a dusty flat-brimmed hat casting a shadow over his face. He watched two men hitch a team of six mules to a supply wagon. Lines weathered his face like cracked leather, and a thick, dark beard covered his jaw.

As Cole watched, the man stepped forward and ran a hand down the leg of one of the lead mules, checking the harness with a practiced touch. He spoke to the driver, who lowered his gaze and nodded in deference.

Yeah, this must be him.

Cole wiped his sweaty palms on his pants and made his way to the camp. A hundred eyes pricked his skin as he crossed the invisible boundary into Travers's domain. The men loading the wagons glanced at him and went back to their work. Cole knew they thought him to be just another dreamer looking to hitch a ride west, but they were wrong.

I'm gonna make it.

He swallowed past a hard knot in his throat and walked directly toward the wagon master, stopping a respectful few feet away.

Once Travers finished his inspection, he turned to Cole. He had the eyes of a man who judged things quickly and accurately—livestock, weather, and other men. For a moment, Cole felt *transparent*, as if Travers could see right through him to the frightened orphan boy beneath the confident posture.

"Sir, my name is Cole Slade." He tipped his hat. "I hear tell you're the man to talk to 'bout headin' to Oregon."

Travers gave Cole a slow look, going over his worn but clean clothes, his sturdy boots, the determined set of his jaw, and the calluses on his large hands.

The silent appraisal lasted an eternity.

"Name's Boone Travers. You heard right," Travers said. "One man's passage runs eight hundred dollars—up front."

Eight hundred dollars. He might as well have said eight thousand. The pouch on his belt might as well be carrying pebbles. Forty-three dollars and sixteen cents. A lifetime of saving, and it amounted to nothing. The hopeful excitement that had carried him all the way here evaporated. His face flushed, blood rushing to his ears.

"Sir, I... I ain't got that kind of money."

Cole *hated* the words and the admission of failure before he had even begun his journey.

"But I pull my weight. Know stock, fix what's broke, shoot straight. I'll earn my keep, sure as sunrise."

Travers let out a sharp sigh. He had clearly heard this speech before.

"Son, every broke soul from here to St. Joe tells me they're a hard worker. This ain't no charity, son. It's business. Gettin' folks to Oregon takes coin."

"I can work as a trail hand, sir, I—"

"No pay, no passage." Travers shook his head. "That's the long and short of it."

He turned away, his attention already shifting back to the wagons, dismissing Cole as if he were no longer there.

The finality of it slammed shut in Cole's face like a closed door. He stood frozen, the noise of the city fading to a dull roar in his ears. The sensation of standing outside a locked gate, of playing a part he hadn't earned, coiled in his gut once more. Just another orphan with empty pockets and big dreams. Luke had told him Kansas would chew a boy up and spit him out, and the first bitter taste of it coated Cole's tongue.

I could go back.

He could swallow his pride and return to Big Cedar with his tail between his legs. Yet, the thought repulsed him so much that it sparked a fresh flicker of defiance in him.

No. He would not go back.

He was about to walk away and figure out some other plan, any other plan, when a violent braying ripped through the air.

The two mules Travers had inspected bucked and kicked, their bodies twisting against the constraints of the harness. The other four caught the fear like a flame catching on dry tinder, and the entire team erupted into a flailing mass of muscles and hooves. The two men handling them shouted and stumbled back, trying desperately to control the lead ropes but failing.

Leather straps groaned and snapped. The heavy wagon tongue jerked violently from side to side. One of the men, a younger fellow with sandy hair, tried to grab a bridle when a rear mule lashed out with its back legs. Hoof thudded against bone. The man went down hard in the mud, clutching his leg, his face contorting in agony. The mules tangled themselves in their own rigging and threatened to tear the entire wagon apart or bolt into the crowded street.

Men shouted and ran, some towards the injured man, others away from the dangerous animals. The controlled order of Boone Travers's camp dissolved into panic.

Cole acted.

An instinct took over that years of handling the stubborn and sometimes volatile animals at Slade's Way had honed. Dropping his pack, he circled wide, avoiding the dangerous kicking zone behind the animals. He fixated on the lead mule.

His voice flowed low and steady, a calming current in the storm of noise. "Easy now... easy, girl... Settle down."

Luke had taught him that an animal's fear fed on a man's panic. You had to be the stillest thing in the tempest.

He kept talking in a meaningless murmur as he slowly closed the distance.

Reaching the side of the lead mule, he extended his hand with his palm down. He let the animal smell it, while his voice continued its hypnotic drone. The mule's ears twitched, its frantic breathing slowing down. Cole laid his hand gently on its neck. He could *feel* the tremors running through the animal's powerful body. He stroked its neck with slow passes from its ears down to its withers. The mule shuddered once, then let out a whooshing breath.

Its head lowered.

The calm spread down the line. The other mules settled, their frantic movements subsiding into twitches and shivers. Cole, still murmuring, moved carefully along the team, untangling a twisted strap here, loosening a harness that was biting into flesh there.

Within a minute, the mules stood still. They were exhausted and trembling, but they no longer threatened anyone.

Cole stepped back. He breathed heavily, his shirt sticking to his back with sweat. The other men stared at him with their mouths agape.

Travers stood with his arms crossed, staring at Cole with an unreadable expression. He must've watched the entire event unfold without saying a word. Well, unless Cole had just been too invested in the mules to notice. Either way, Travers pushed himself away from the wagon he'd been leaning against and walked over to where his men were supporting the man who'd gotten hurt.

Travers examined the man's leg. "It's busted. Get him to the doc. Tell him to set it right and put it on my account."

The men nodded and half-carried, half-dragged the groaning man away. Travers watched them go, then his piercing gray eyes turned back to Cole. The older man walked over and stopped right in front of him.

Cole met his gaze, his breathing returning to normal. He had done what needed to be done. It was as simple as that. He expected no praise or reward. The satisfaction of helping was enough for him.

"You got a name for handlin' stock," Travers said. "Where'd a pup like you pick that up?"

"We had mules at Slade's Way, sir." Cole smiled. "The orphanage where I was raised. Stubborn critters, most of 'em."

"That's one word for it." Travers glanced at the now docile team of mules, then back at Cole. "Lost a hand just now. Man busted his leg clean through. He ain't crossin' no prairie."

Please say what I think you'll say!

"Trail hand earns his passage, room, board, and ten dollars come Oregon—if we make it. Else, you get paid in blisters."

Cole nodded. "Thank you, sir."

"It's hard, dirty work. Up 'fore dawn, bed after dusk. You'll be wet, hungry, bone-tired. You'll fight mud, river, and mountain. And you'll answer to me, every step. You still fixin' to head west?"

Relief flooded through Cole with such power it almost buckled his knees. He had a place and he had *earned* it. The feeling was more valuable than any amount of money.

"Yes, sir." Cole clenched his jaw. "I do."

"The spot is yours then. We pull out at dawn, day after tomorrow. Find a place to stow your gear. You can sleep in the barn over there for the night."

He gestured with his chin toward a weathered structure on the edge of the property. He started to turn away, then paused.

"Slade, you said?"

"Yes, sir. Cole Slade."

Travers nodded once more, as if filing the name away. "Don't make me regret this, Slade."

With that, he walked away, already shouting orders to get the mules re-hitched and the loading finished.

Cole stood there for a moment, letting it all sink in. A genuine smile spread across his face, the first since he had left Big Cedar.

He walked over and picked up his pack. As he turned toward the barn, two other young men approached him. They looked about his age, maybe a year or two older, and wore the same trail-worn clothes as the other hands. One was lean and wiry with a perpetual sneer on his lips. The other had a broader frame and a scar over his left eye.

The sneering one stepped in front of Cole, blocking his path to the barn. "What's the hurry, mule-whisperer?"

Cole's hand tightened on the strap of his pack. "Can I help you?"

"Name's Elias. That there's Silas. Wyatt is a friend of ours."

"What's that got to do with me?"

"He was s'posed to ride this train. Now he's busted up, and you're sittin' in his saddle." Elias took a step closer. "We don't take kindly to that. Don't take kindly to *you* neither."

Cole looked from Elias's hostile face to Silas's quiet glare. He held his ground, his posture as straight and unyielding as Luke had taught him.

"I didn't ask for his spot," Cole said. "I'm just here to do a job."

Elias let out a cold chuckle. "Well, you best mind your step, greenhorn."

Chapter Three

May 3rd, 1852

Kansas, Missouri

Shuddering tremors of exhaustion from the horse—a bony gelding named Ghost for his pale coat—ran up the reins and into June's own aching arms. His ribs heaved with every ragged breath, his sweat-lathered hide flooding with a grimy sheen under the oppressive Missouri sun.

They had been riding hard for two days straight, pushing through the night with only the moon for a guide, stopping only when Ghost threatened to collapse beneath her. She knew the feeling. Adrenaline and fatigue had pulled her own body into a taut wire, her frayed nerves threatening to snap.

Behind them, Benton County unfurled like a bad dream she tried desperately to outrun. *Jax* lurked back there. Or, more terrifyingly, he hunted for her somewhere on the road between there and here.

She urged Ghost forward, her heels nudging his depleted flanks.

Kansas rose from the plains ahead in a smear of smoke, soot, and people. The perfect place to hide and get lost in the crowd before the real journey began.

As she rode, every rustle in the tall grass sent a quiver through her core. She'd glance back over her shoulder, expecting to see the Thorns cresting the last hill. Jax, Mercy, Griffin, Clay. They had been her family, the only one she'd ever known. Now they'd become the monsters in her story.

Her hand drifted to the pistol tucked into the waistband of her skirt. For June, who'd never killed before, it would do little against four people—one of whom had lost his soul—but it beat going in barehanded. At least she could put up a fight before they took her, or make sure they never could.

As she entered the city's sprawling outskirts, the overwhelming roar of civilization replaced the open country's quiet menace. The noise assaulted her. Wagons creaked, oxen bellowed, men shouted, and a thousand different conversations blended into a meaningless cacophony. The smell was worse. A thick stew of mud, manure, sweat, and cooking fires clogged her throat.

The gateway to her promised land stank like hell's back door.

She guided Ghost toward her first stop, a farrier's shop operating from a grimy lean-to with a plume of black smoke rising from its chimney. Dismounting hurt. Her legs had adjusted to the protection of boys' britches, and her thighs under the despised dress ached whenever it touched something. The rough-spun fabric, a drab brown she'd chosen to blend in, chafed her skin and draped over her like a costume for a part she had no idea how to play.

Still, a lone woman wearing pants invited trouble, while one in a dress appeared poor and desperate, one of a thousand others. It was the lesser of two evils.

The farrier—a barrel-chested man with arms like tree limbs and a beard stained with tobacco juice—checked out Ghost then her.

"Lookin' to sell?" He spat to the side. "He's been rode hard, near to foundered. Ain't worth much but dogmeat."

"He got me here," June said.

She hated the man's dismissive tone and the way his eyes lingered on her chest. Having to part with Ghost scorched the back of her throat. The gelding had been her only confidant ever since she'd fled Benton, his steady presence comforting her in the terrifying dark. Selling him stung like a betrayal, but Jax would recognize Ghost from a mile away, and June just couldn't risk it.

The farrier offered her a pittance. She haggled with all the skill she'd honed in countless back alleys and crooked markets. They settled on a price that still insulted her but exceeded what he'd first offered. He counted out the coins into her palm, the thump of metal against her skin making her sick.

As he led Ghost away, the horse turned his head and looked back at her with his large eyes. For a heart-stopping moment, June wanted to snatch the money back, grab his reins, and ride.

But ride where?

Every road back to Jax. She swallowed the lump in her throat, shoved the coins deep into a hidden pocket sewn into her petticoat, and turned her back.

She had to find the wagon master trail hands talked about in saloons all through her road here. Boone Travers. Everyone spoke his name with a mix of respect and fear, which must've been a good sign. Men who inspired fear often got things done.

She made her way through the throng, clutching the small satchel that held her few belongings.

The dress constantly irritated her skin and reminded her of her vulnerability. Underneath it, the spirit of June Crow—who could pick a pocket clean before the mark knew he'd been jostled, and fight with a ferocity that surprised men twice her size—blazed as strong as ever. But—as much as she hated it—

she needed this performance of femininity to shield her, no matter how much it suffocated her.

A commotion up ahead made her pause.

A crowd was gathering near a large encampment, where the pristine white canvas of a dozen wagons gleamed against the landscape. This had to be Travers's company. A team of mules created the disturbance, their bodies bucking and their screams tearing through the air in a panicked frenzy. Their harness straps ensnared them, their powerful legs kicking out with deadly force. Men shouted, scrambling to get out of the way.

Then a young man moved toward the terrified animals.

He looked about her age and circled them calmly. The low murmur of his voice remained unclear, yet its calming effect rippled through the air toward her. He was tall and lean, with shaggy dark hair that fell into his eyes. He had the lanky look of a boy still growing into a man's frame, but he moved with a competence that belied his age.

Her first thought questioned his motives. Why was he showing off? People who drew attention to themselves invited danger. They made others look at them, and June wanted to stay invisible.

She watched as he murmured to the lead mule, his hand steady on its trembling neck. The effect spread quickly, a wave of calm passing through the team. She'd seen a thousand acts of violence and cruelty in her life, but never such a soft approach.

It reminded her, with a sickening lurch, of Jax.

Not the act itself, but the contrast. A year ago, outside a small farming community, a farmer's wagon had blocked their path. Jax had tipped the wagon over, sending crates of chickens scattering and screaming. When the old farmer protested, Jax had just laughed and kicked the man's legs out from under him, leaving him sprawling in the mud. Jax defined himself with such actions, equating strength with the suffering of others.

This boy sought to mend. Create order from chaos instead of the other way around. The thought confused her, and she pushed it away. He'd simply introduced a new unknown into her life, which already overflowed with them.

Let him play the hero. I have to focus on myself.

She needed a moment. To breathe, think, and let the hammering of her heart subside before she approached a man like Boone Travers.

She spotted a saloon across the street, its doors swinging open and shut like a beating heart, spilling out noise and the scent of stale beer. A less-than-ideal place for a lone woman, but public. Paradoxically, she'd find the greatest safety in a crowd, where a scream would reach other ears, even if those ears chose to dismiss it.

She crossed the street, dodging a freight wagon whose driver cursed her without even looking. Pushing through the swinging doors, she stepped into the gloom. Thick smoke and the smell of unwashed men clogged the air. A scrawny man played a piano in the corner with more enthusiasm than skill. Dozens of faces, all male, turned to look at her as she entered. Their eyes prodded her like physical touches. Appraising. Dismissing. Desiring.

She kept her gaze fixed on the long wooden bar and walked toward it with her back straight, projecting a confidence that sat on her like a borrowed coat.

"Sarsaparilla," she said.

The bartender—a bald man with a stained apron and oily hair—extended his palm.

She sighed and slid a coin onto the sticky bar top.

He grunted and slid a glass of the fizzy liquid toward her. She took it and retreated to an empty table in the corner, which offered a view of the entire room, including the entrance. Always knowing her exits and watching for threats had become a habit long ago.

She took a slow sip, the sweet taste coating her tongue. She tried to steady her breathing, to push the image of Jax's face from her mind. His obsession with her consumed him. She knew that now. What she had once mistaken for affection or protectiveness had become a twisted obsession that wrapped around her like barbed wire. He considered her *his*. Something he had found and shaped. As if she were his property.

She was only too aware that Jax Rae did *not* take kindly to his property walking away.

Her mind spiraled inward, and only the saloon owner's shadow falling across her table jolted her back to the room. A portly man stood before her—his clothes looking a little too fine for the establishment he ran, and a fake gold tooth glinting when he smiled.

"This ain't no place for a sweet thing like you to be sittin' all by her lonesome." He pulled up a chair and sat down. "Unless you're lookin' for work?"

June's blood ran cold.

She knew exactly what kind of 'work' he meant. She'd seen girls younger than her get trapped in places like this for men to use until they lost all will to live.

"Ain't that kinda work I'm after."

"A girl that travels needs protection. Steady income. I can provide that. A roof over your head, good meals—"

"As long as I make the clients happy, right?"

"See, you get it." He leaned closer, his foul breath washing over her. "You'd make a fortune."

A hot surge scorched the cold knot in her gut. Her hand twitched, creeping to the knife in her skirt. She could have it out and at his throat before he could blink. The Thorns had taught her that. But that would bring the whole town down on her. It would be the end of her escape before it even began.

"I said no."

He put his doughy hand on her arm. "Now, don't be so quick, darlin'. Ain't no shame in—"

"The lady said no," a calm voice said from beside them.

June looked up, her eyes landing on the boy from the street. The one who'd handled the mules. He stood there with a serious expression, his dark eyes cutting into the saloon owner.

I didn't even hear him approach.

The owner looked him up and down. "Ain't none o' your business, boy. Git."

"Well, I reckon I'm makin' it my business." The young man kept his shoulders relaxed and his hands loose. "Now, why don't you leave her alone 'fore we have a problem."

The saloon owner stared at the boy, then at June's stony face, and seemed to weigh his options. This young man's slight frame suggested little threat, but a core of absolute resolve emanated from him that must've given the owner pause. With a disgruntled sigh, the man pushed himself to his feet.

"Have it your way." He gave June one last, greedy look. "Your loss."

He turned and lumbered back toward the bar.

The tightness in her shoulders eased for a split second before a hot flush climbed her neck, and her jaw clenched. She fought her own battles. Being 'saved' by a man just put you in his debt, and she refused all debt.

She stood up and grabbed her satchel. "I didn't need your help."

The boy looked taken aback. "Fella was outta line."

"I can handle myself." She turned to leave, wanting nothing more than to put this entire encounter behind her.

"Wait." He took a step after her. "I just... I'm Cole. Cole Slade."

He offered the name as if extending a gift. To June, it represented a liability. A name forged a connection, and those became chains.

"Thanks, Cole Slade," she said, already turning to leave, "but I don't need an escort."

His eyes darkened for a moment before a shutter fell over his expression. Good. Let him be hurt. He *should* think she was an ungrateful shrew. It was safer that way. People kept their distance from a mean spirit. The orphanage had hammered that lesson into her.

She pushed through the swinging doors and back out into the street.

She needed to find a place to sleep, a lodging house that wouldn't ask too many questions. The wagon train would leave soon, and she *would* be on it. Alone. Unbeholden. A ghost disappearing into the vast west. And no one—neither the ghost of Jax Rae nor some do-gooding boy named Cole Slade—would get in her way.

Chapter Four

The night of May 4th, 1852

Kansas, Missouri

The barn Boone Travers had gestured to earlier loomed before him, its cavernous space rising like a cathedral of rough-hewn timber, the air inside smelling of hay and livestock. Slivers of moonlight pierced the gaps between the wallboards, painting spectral stripes across the dusty floor. The scene opposed the clean dormitories of Slade's Way, but, as Cole spread his bedroll in a mound of hay, a sense of peace settled over him.

I can't believe I'm only getting here now. Must've lost more time in the saloon than I thought.

He lay back, lacing his hands behind his head, and stared up into the shadowy rafters where swallows nested.

The way the girl in the saloon had dismissed him even after he'd helped her stung him. He'd seen her fear when that brigand had cornered her, and he'd stepped in because that was what Luke had taught him to do. You didn't stand by while a wolf sank its teeth into a lamb. But she'd reacted with ice in her voice and narrow eyes, as if he had joined the threat instead of opposing it.

Cole had spent his life trying to be helpful, a mediator, what Luke had called 'a force for good.' Today, for the first time ever, he'd experienced such a thorough rejection of his help.

She never even told me her name.

Well, to each their own. He had nothing to do with her problems. Plenty of those on his own plate. A job. Proving to Travers that he'd made the right choice. Cole had to be the best trail hand this side of the Missouri.

He closed his eyes. The sounds of the camp—a distant cough, the soft nickering of a horse, the faint, rhythmic clang from the blacksmith's forge as the smith worked late—lulled him to sleep.

***

He drifted in that hazy space between wakefulness and dreams when the shock came.

The violence of cold water splashing against his face woke him. As if a river had risen and crashed down upon him. It sluiced over his face, into his ears, down his neck, and soaked his shirt and bedroll in an instant. He gasped, sputtering, his body convulsing from the shock as he shot upright. For a disoriented second, he thought the barn roof had caved in during a freak storm.

Then the laughter came.

Mean-spirited chuckles boomed from the darkness just beyond his makeshift bed. As his eyes adjusted, he made out three figures standing over him. In the faint moonlight, he recognized the sneering face of Elias and the hulking shape of Silas. The third man held an empty wooden bucket, dripping the last of its contents onto the hay.

"Rise an' shine, golden boy," Elias spat the word with a venom that surprised Cole with its intensity. "Figured you needed a proper washin' 'fore your first day's work."

Cole frowned. At Slade's Way, 'orphan' signified a bond that tied them all together. It held no shame. Here, the mouth of this sneering man had turned it into a weapon. An insult to disgrace him and reduce him to something lesser. An offense to Luke and every boy who had ever found a home within those walls.

Cole got to his feet. Water drenched him, sending shivers through his body as hay clung to his wet clothes, but he rose to his full height, his posture as ramrod straight as Luke had always insisted.

He towered over Elias. "There ain't no call for this."

As much as he wanted to knock Elias' teeth out, honoring Luke's lessons came first. A gentleman rose above conflict, and Cole was trying with all the strength he had to do just that. Even as his large hands curled into fists at his sides.

"Oh, there's call, alright." Elias took a step closer. "You come stridin' in here, actin' the hero with them mules, like you're somethin' special. That don't sit right."

The third man, the one with the bucket, snickered. "Shoulda kept your nose outta other folks' business."

"Wyatt broke his own leg." Cole clenched his jaw. "Ain't got nothin' to do with me."

"You're a handout, that's all," Silas scoffed. "Boone must be soft on strays. We sure ain't."

He shoved Cole hard in the chest.

Cole stumbled backward, his boots slipping in the wet hay. He caught his balance, but something inside him snapped. He hadn't come all this way, left the only home he'd ever known, to allow bullies who thought his past made him weak to push him around in the dark.

He shoved back.

He put the strength of his shoulders and back into it, a strength he'd built over years of chopping wood and hauling water. Silas went staggering back several feet, tripping over a loose pile of hay and landing hard on his backside.

For a moment, only the sound of Silas' surprised grunt filled the air. Then, Silas scrambled to his feet with a roar.

"You're gonna pay for that, boy," Silas said.

Elias lunged. Cole sidestepped, and Elias's wild punch whistled past his ear. Silas grabbed for Cole's arms from behind, but Cole twisted, shrugging off the grip. The third man stared from the side, clutching his bucket.

The scrap descended into a clumsy dance in the near darkness.

They flailed around in a bunch of thrashing limbs and grunts of effort. Cole lacked a brawler's skill—Luke had forbidden fighting at the orphanage—but a deep well of strength flowed through him, and a righteous fire in his chest lent him power. He landed a solid blow to Silas' gut, doubling him over with a wheeze, but Elias tackled him at the waist, and they both went down into the hay.

A fist glanced off Cole's cheekbone as he got his hands on Elias' shirt and pushed him off, the cheap whiskey on the man's breath stinging his nostrils. Silas kicked his ribs, the jarring blows keeping him down on the ground even as Elias stood up. He was losing the fight, and he knew it.

I need to get back up and—

"ENOUGH!"

The voice cracked like a whip, roaring with command that cut through the grunting and scuffling and froze every man in place. Travers held a lantern in the massive barn doorway, taking in the entire scuffle with narrow eyes.

Icy fingers, far more chilling than the bucket of water, seized Cole. It was over. His grand adventure on the Oregon Trail had lasted less than twelve hours. Travers had given him one instruction—*Don't make me regret this, Slade*—and Cole had failed in the most spectacular way possible. Yes, Silas had pushed first, but Cole had responded. If he had just remained calm, as Luke had taught him, the three bullies would've likely walked away. Instead, he had sunk right down into the muck with them.

Elias scrambled off him, hastily trying to brush himself down and adopt an expression of injured innocence. Silas and the other man backed away, their faces pale in the lantern light. Cole pushed himself up to a sitting position, the wet hay scratching his skin, his head facing down.

Travers strolled in and stopped in the middle of the group. "Someone wants to tell me what in the Sam Hill is goin' on in my barn?"

Elias pointed at Cole. "Sir, it was him! Slade here jumped us, no warnin'. We was just checkin' on the stock, honest."

Cole's head snapped up. The audacity of the bald-faced lie stunned him. He looked at Elias, then at Travers. He opened his mouth to protest, to tell the truth, but then closed it. What was the point? His word against three. As if Travers would believe a newcomer he'd hired out of a moment of necessity over seasoned hands he already knew.

Travers glanced at Cole. "Slade? Is that how it happened?"

Since Travers had asked, he might as well try telling the truth.

"They doused me while I was sleepin'." Cole gestured to his soaked clothes and the damp patch of hay. "Mocked me. Shoved me first, and I pushed back."

He refused to whine and point fingers. Cole had stated the facts as they had happened and took his share of the responsibility for the fight. It was only fair. He *had* lowered himself to their level and would accept the consequences and braced himself for the inevitable words: *You're off the train.*

Travers' eyes flashed from Cole's drenched form to the empty bucket in the third man's arms, then to the shifting eyes of the other three men.

He focused on the third man. "What's your name?"

The man stared at his boots. "Jed, sir."

"Jed," Travers said. "Well, Jed—you're done. You and your gear off my train come sunup. You'll get what I owe, then I want you gone. I run a wagon train, not no baby corral."

Jed's head shot up. "But... it was Elias's idea!"

"Don't give a damn whose bright idea it was. You held the bucket. You're out."

"But I—"

"Shut up! I ain't interested."

The man gulped and closed his mouth.

Travers turned his glare on Elias and Silas. "As for you two— you're walkin' the edge of a cliff, and I won't blink if you fall. You do your job, keep your traps shut, and you stay the hell away from Slade. One more sideways glance, and you're hoofin' it back to Missouri. Got me?"

"Yes, sir," they mumbled in unison.

"Now get out of my sight. All of you." Travers gestured the lantern at the barn door. "Go find a place to sleep where you won't cause any more trouble."

Elias shot Cole a look of pure hatred as he scurried past him, one that promised this wasn't over. Then they vanished back into the darkness.

Cole sat alone with Travers in the quiet of the dark barn. The tension rushed from his body with such sudden immensity that his head swam. He'd kept his job. Travers had valued his honesty. He slowly got to his feet, still dripping onto the floor.

"Thank you, sir," he said quietly.

Travis grunted and set the lantern down on a nearby crate. "Don't thank me."

"You ain't sent me packin'."

"I need a man who can handle mules more than I need a man who acts like one." He looked Cole over. "You know, it only just dawned on me you said you were an orphan."

"Yes, sir. I was raised at Slade's Way."

"It was a good place, yes?"

"Yes, sir. The man who runs it, Luke Slade, is a good man."

Travers studied Cole's face in the lamplight. "I was an orphan myself. Left on a church step in St. Louis. Bounced from one place to another. Some not so good."

Cole stared at him.

Boone Travers—the tough, self-sufficient, respected wagon master—came from the same world as Cole. The revelation re-contextualized everything he'd assumed about Travers. The man's hardness must've developed as a shell over a core of self-reliance. It made sense. Only one Luke Slade lived in this world, and Cole had had the fortune to grow up with him.

A blink of genuine connection sparked in Cole's chest, a sense that another soul would understand him on the harsh path of the Oregon Trail.

"You gotta learn somethin', son," Travers said. "Out here, on the trail, a fight like this is more than a fight."

"What do you mean?"

"If you gotta spend all your time lookin' over your back out of fear for your fellow trail hands, you ain't gon' notice a rattler or that a river's current is faster than it looks."

Cole sighed. "I can't stop them from hating me."

"I'm not sayin' you can, but you need to be careful about where your focus lies." Travers smiled. "I ain't got no idea what the insult was, but I reckon it was bad?"

Cole looked down.

"You gotta get that chip off your shoulder, son. Your past doesn't matter out here. What you can do, what you can endure, how you keep your head when things get rough... that's all that's important."

Cole nodded. "I'll try."

Travers picked up the lantern. "Get some sleep, Slade. You got a long day tomorrow."

Chapter Five

The morning of May 5th, 1852

Kansas, Missouri

Cole's cheekbone throbbed.

He'd woken before the first hint of gray light touched the sky, his body stiff from the damp hay and the fight. But as he stood in the pre-dawn chaos of Travers's camp, he pushed the ache aside, its presence fading to a minor thrum in his muscles. A sense of belonging settled in his chest, so new and fragile he cupped it gently, like a fledgling bird he feared might startle and fly away.

Cole's responsibilities were simple for now. Keep the mules calm, check tethers, be ready to lend a hand. He did so with a focused intensity, running his hands over the leather, speaking to the animals in the same low murmur he'd used the day before. Elias's glare stabbed into his back from across the camp, but Cole focused only on his work.

A call went up, and the nervous energy of the camp coalesced.

Travers climbed onto the tongue of a wagon.

"Listen up! Name's Boone Travers. For the next five, maybe six months, I'm your wagon master. That means what I say goes, no ifs, ands, or buts. I've run this trail six times now, and I know what it takes to reach the end with your hide still intact."

Travers scanned the crowd—hopeful farmers, grim-faced prospectors, and wide-eyed children clinging to their mothers' skirts.

"This ain't no Sunday stroll. We're looking at more than *two thousand miles* of the roughest terrain known to man. God did *not* intend for us to traverse this trail! It *will* try to starve you, freeze you, and drown you. It'll send sickness, snakes, and storms. You will get tired. You will get scared. You will get angry at your neighbor for the smallest thing."

Cole blinked. Travers sure wasn't holding back.

"Until we get to Oregon, you are not individuals! We are a train. We move together, we work together, and if need be, we fight together. You see a man's wagon stuck in the mud, you put your shoulder to it. You see a woman who's lost her stock, you share your water. You look out for each other's children as if they were your own. Selfishness is a disease that can kill a wagon train faster than cholera. Do you understand me?"

A chorus of *'Yes, sir!'* exploded from the crowd.

Luke had taught them this exact same lesson at Slade's Way, just on a much smaller scale. Community. Shared responsibility. The idea that strength lay in unity. Cole had really made a good decision joining this train.

Travers laid out the rules of the trail—the march order, watch duties, the signals for circling the wagons. Cole tried to pay attention and memorize every detail, but his mind kept drifting. He scanned the edges of the crowd. Years at the orphanage had instilled in him the habit of watching the fringes for trouble.

That's when he saw the girl from the saloon.

Two figures had pinned her against the wall in the narrow gap between the back of the land office and a livery stable.

Even from this distance, Cole could see the men's aggressive postures, how they leaned in to block any possibility of escape.

A flash of heat shot through him. Her ungrateful words from yesterday repeated in his ears. *'I can handle myself.'* Clearly, she couldn't. A part of him—the petty one that bristled from her rejection—wanted to turn away. Her problems had nothing to do with him, she'd made that abundantly clear. He should just focus on Boone's instructions, on his job.

Of course, I can't.

Her body went rigid, her back pressing flat against the rough-hewn planks as if trying to merge with them. One of the men's hands shot out and grabbed her arm. In that moment, the sting in Cole's chest vanished to the unshakeable bedrock of his upbringing. *'You don't stand by.'*

The voice in his head belonged to Luke.

With a last glance at Travers, who still spoke from his perch, Cole slipped away from the supply wagon. He moved quietly, circling around the edge of the assembly. As he drew closer, the brigands' voices drifted to him.

"Aw, we just want a bit of fun, darlin'. Nothin' to fuss over," one of them said.

The man was burly with a grimy beard and the rank smell of stale whiskey clinging to him, and his tone made Cole's skin crawl.

"Just a lil kiss to see us off right." The other one—a short fellow with ginger hair—laughed. "For luck."

"Leave me alone." Her voice trembled low in her throat, her knuckles white where she fisted her skirt.

The burly one clenched her cheeks. "Don't be like that, now. You're gonna give us that kiss—an' plenty more after."

Cole stopped a few feet away. "She said to leave her alone."

The two men turned, their expressions shifting from predatory leering to annoyance. They were likely trail hands from a different, less-organized outfit. Drifters looking for a last bit of trouble before heading into the wilderness.

"This ain't your affair, friend." The burly one clicked his tongue. "Take a walk."

Cole's heart pounded, his ears ringing, and he held his hands open at his sides. Two opponents stood in front of him, and he'd learned last night how quickly that could go wrong. This had to end without a fight. He needed something to make them back down.

An idea bloomed in his mind.

He sighed and shook his head. "Honestly, dear, I told you this town was full o' lowlifes, but you had to go wanderin' off."

The ginger glared at him. "What are you on about?"

Cole scowled back. "Unhand my betrothed."

"Betrothed?" The burly one jeered. "Ain't look like she's betrothed."

"And you don't look like no gentleman, yet here we are." Cole took another step. "We're with Boone Travers's outfit, and we roll out in ten. You can walk away now, or explain to Boone why you was puttin' your paws on a lady in his camp. Your pick."

Travers' name did what Cole's presence failed to do. The two men exchanged nervous glances. Cole could tell what was going on in their heads. Travers' reputation preceded him, and tangling with a man like him over a woman who was spoken for was plain stupid.

The burly one released the girl's arm and shoved her at Cole. "Keep your woman on a shorter leash."

Muttering curses under their breath, the two turned and disappeared back into the teeming throng of the street.

Cole braced himself for another explosion, for the same sharp-tongued anger she'd shown him in the saloon. He expected her to rail at him for his presumption, for the outrageous lie he'd just told.

She wrapped her arms around herself and looked down.

Her face went pale in the growing light of dawn, and a stray lock of her dark brown hair fell across her cheek. Her petite frame and short stature made her look so young and fragile that Cole couldn't believe she had the core of tempered steel he'd witnessed yesterday in those doe eyes.

He approached her. "Are you alright?"

She nodded.

"Once again, my name is Cole Slade." He smiled, hoping for a different result this time.

She inhaled. "June Crow."

"Well, it's nice meeting you, June." He rubbed the back of his head. "I ought to be getting back. Travers will be finishing up by now."

Looking everywhere but him, she left the alley before him.

Cole followed her with a thousand questions on his mind.

Who was she? Why was she alone? Why did trouble find her so easily?

He kept his mouth shut, however. He had a feeling questions would be as welcome as a rattlesnake in a bedroll.

On the main street, the first wagons creaked forward. People scrambled to their places, shouting last-minute instructions. Travers had mounted his horse and directed the flow from the front of the line.

To Cole's surprise, June walked straight up to Travers' horse, stopping at his stirrup and forcing the trail boss to look down at her.

"Mr. Travers." She inclined her head. "My name is June Crow. I need passage on your train."

Travers glanced down at her. "That'll be eight hundred dollars, miss. Up front."

Cole's heart sank for her. The stammered explanation of why she needed to go would come next, the offer to work, and the inevitable rejection that would crush her soul. It would look the same as it had for him, and he wished he could spare her the pain somehow.

June reached into a hidden pocket in her drab dress and pulled out a wad of cash she'd tied with a piece of twine.

Cole's jaw dropped. He hadn't seen that much money in one place in his entire life. The worn and crumpled bills formed a thick roll that promised substantial payment.

Travers stared at the money, then at June's pale face. Reaching down, he took the money and counted it with a practiced thumb. "This is the right amount, but I have a rule, Miss Crow. No single women travel with my train."

The color drained from June's cheeks. "What? Why?"

"Ain't safe. Ain't proper. Brings trouble both ways." Travers offered her the money back. "I'm responsible for this whole outfit, and a lone gal just ain't worth the grief."

Cole watched her pupils dilate, her throat working as she swallowed. Her composure crumbled. Whatever chased her must've made Kansas an impossible place to stay. All of Cole's questions about her identity and where she got the money vanished from his mind. A person in desperate need of help stood in front of him, and he had to help her.

But how?

Travis had said he wouldn't accept a lone woman, which meant that her salvation lay in the lie Cole had said in the alley. He'd have to gamble on the man he'd talked to last night—the one who understood what it meant to be alone and in trouble—to value fairness over blind adherence to rules.

Cole stepped up to Travers' stirrup. "Sir, maybe there's a way 'round it."

Travers's brows drew together. "Go on."

"You said no single women. Well... she don't have to be." He took a deep breath. "Let her ride as my intended."

Travers looked from Cole's earnest face to June's stunned one. Cole's lungs burned. His plea had come from a desire to help, but he'd put his own standing with the trail boss on the line nonetheless. June trembled beside him.

Finally, Travers let out a weary sigh and ran his hand over his thick beard. "I hired you to wrangle stock, Slade, not play chaperone to some gal you fibbed over before we've even lost sight of the river."

"Luke raised me better'n to turn my back on someone needin' help."

"Well, Miss Crow, you heard the boy's idea." Travers looked at her. "You willin' to go along with that?"

June swallowed hard. "Yes."

"Then fine. You ride with us under that lie." He scowled at them both. "But listen close—any funny business, any drama, and I drop the both of you at the next fort. Got it?"

"Yes, sir," Cole said.

"Yes."

"Good." Travers pulled on his reins, turning his horse. "Slade, get to your mules. Miss Crow, find a spot for your things in the supply wagon, of which your... intended is in charge."

With that, he rode off, shouting orders to get the train moving in earnest.

Chapter Six

May 8th, 1852

Kansas River Ferry Crossing

The past three days had been a special kind of hell, as she endured grinding hours that bled into moments of heart-stopping panic. The rhythmic squeak and groan of the wagon wheels counted down the seconds of June's life. By day, the sun beat down on the white canvas cover of the supply wagon, turning the space beneath it into a sweltering oven. By night, the prairie pressed in, the darkness swarming with a thousand phantom threats, while each rustle of the tall grass brought her Jax's footsteps.

June drove the heavy supply wagon, a task she had volunteered for with an eagerness that had earned her a surprised look from Cole. Of course, he didn't understand. Being in charge of this lumbering beast meant she had a purpose. A reason to stay separate. It put a shield of responsibility between her and the prying eyes of the other travelers.

The Marlowe family, with their loving glances and their cherubic daughter Lily, made her skin itch. The two widowed sisters, Savannah and Pearl, with their whispered gossip and knowing smiles, pierced her skin like a physical intrusion. They all looked at her, then at Cole, their faces softening with sentimentality that branded her.

Maintaining the charade exhausted her more than the trail itself.

The word *'betrothed'* sat like a bitter stone in her mouth, binding her to a boy who represented everything she was not.

47

Open, trusting, and pathologically helpful. He slept on his bedroll next to the wagon. He'd bring her a tin plate of food from the communal fire and smile when she retreated into the wagon to eat alone.

She hated his quiet decency.

The way he talked to the mules in a calming rumble. How he conversed with Joe Marlowe about crop rotation. The gentle smile he gave five-year-old Lily when she offered him a wilted wildflower.

Each act of kindness judged June's life, showing her a stark illustration of a world she had never been allowed to inhabit. His goodness cast a spotlight that forced her further into shadow. A cold knot formed in her stomach at the thought of him witnessing her true nature—the thief, the liar, the girl who had stood by while Jax did terrible things—and his mouth twisting at the sight of her.

So, she kept him at a distance with a wall of silence and sharp-edged glares. It protected them both.

Vigilance hummed inside her like a taut wire.

Every rider on the horizon sent a jolt of ice through her veins. She would grip the worn leather reins until her knuckles bleached white. Then the rider would turn out to be a lone trapper or a scout from another train, and the tension would recede, leaving her hollow and shaky.

Jax hunted with *chilling* patience.

He would pursue her without end and likely stalked the prairie somewhere behind them. The three days she had put between herself and Kansas was a meaningless distance. The head start merely postponed a race with an inevitable end.

The wide and brown water of the Kansas River flowed sluggishly under the afternoon sun. A handful of other, smaller wagon trains already crowded the riverbank, a chaotic jumble of wagons, livestock, and frustrated people waiting their turn for the single, slow-moving flatboat that served as a ferry.

Travers halted the train.

June pulled the supply wagon to a stop, the muscles in her shoulders and back screaming in protest. The waiting frayed her nerves more than any part of the journey. It meant being stationary. A sitting target. She chewed on the inside of her lip, scanning the disorganized camps around them, cataloging faces, and looking for any sign of the features she sought to escape.

Her eyes fell on Cole.

He swung off his horse, stretching his long limbs, his shaggy hair falling into his eyes. He swiped it away with an impatient gesture, his dark brown eyes widening as he took in the scene. His posture conveyed the thrill of an unfolding adventure. To June, the scene presented another cage with a different set of bars.

Then, the chaos notched up.

A sharp crack echoed across the riverbank like a rifle shot. An overloaded wagon from one of the other groups tipped, its axle giving way under the strain. A woman screamed. The wagon groaned, swayed, and then crashed onto its side with a sickening splintering of wood. Barrels, crates, and sacks of flour tumbled into the mud.

June pulled her hat lower and made herself smaller.

Don't look. Don't get involved.

E.J. WEST

Trouble in another camp had nothing to do with them. Drawing attention was the last thing she wanted.

Cole jogged to the disaster before the wagon had fully settled.

Her grip tightened on the reins. "Idiot."

He drew the attention of the crows. People pointed at him and, by extension, at the train he belonged to. At her. They would inevitably look at her, the sullen girl he was engaged to. He painted a target on their backs—on *her* back—all for the sake of strangers.

Her jaw tightened as she watched him.

He reached the overturned wagon and directed the panicking family with the same infuriatingly calm voice he'd used on the mules. He organized a handful of gawking men, putting them to work lifting the heavy wagon bed while he scrambled underneath to assess the damage.

A memory sliced through her like a shard of glass lodged under a fingernail.

It had happened last spring, on a road rutted with mud. The Thorns had come upon a homesteader's stuck wagon, its wheel sunk to the hub. The farmer, a man with a weathered face and pleading eyes, had begged for help.

Jax had laughed.

He'd dismounted, swaggering toward the wagon, and instead of helping, he'd placed his shoulder against the side and pushed. To tip it. Mercy and Clay had joined in, laughing as the wagon crashed over, spilling seed corn and tools into the muck. The farmer's wife had cried.

June had stood by her horse as the farmer had asked why.

50

Jax had only said, *'Because I can.'*

As if that had explained everything. In Jax's world, it had. To him, power justified itself. He'd then kicked the farmer's legs out from under him, leaving the man to flounder in the mud.

Cole contrasted that completely.

He knelt under the broken wagon, working alongside the distraught farmer. He tried to mend the broken pieces instead of shattering something to prove his own might. People watched him with admiration. The farmer from the other wagon clapped him on the shoulder. One of the women from their own train, Lenore Marlowe, pointed him out to her husband with a smile on her face.

June didn't understand it.

Kindness was weakness. Helping someone made you a fool. A mark for someone stronger to exploit. Yet here, these people looked at Cole's selfless act and saw *strength*. They respected him for it. That foreign notion, so contrary to every survival instinct she possessed, made her head spin.

As if she were trying to read a book in a language she'd never seen before.

It took the better part of an hour, but they managed to right the wagon and cobble together a temporary repair for the axle, enough to get it onto the ferry. Cole finally emerged, covered in mud but with a look of deep satisfaction on his face. He wiped his hands on his pants and headed back toward their train.

He walked up to her. Axle's patched up. They'll limp along to the fort, sure as sunrise."

June glared at him. "Why can't you just keep your nose outta other folks' troubles?"

He blinked as if he hadn't heard her correctly. "What?"

"Don't play dumb." She kept her voice low so others would overhear nothing. "You think this is some kind of Sunday school pageant? You runnin' around, playin' the hero, gettin' everyone to look at you? To look at *us*?"

"They were in a bad way, June. That wagon was busted clean through."

"Weren't *our* wagon!" She leaned down from the driver's seat. "Weren't our mess! Crossin' this land, makin' it west—it's 'bout watchin' your own back. Ain't no room for chasin' after every poor soul with a broke-down rig. Every minute jawin' or helpin' gets you noticed. Folks knowin' your face. That's danger you just invited in for supper."

He stared at her as if he were trying to solve a difficult puzzle. "Ain't you ever lent a hand 'cause it was right? 'cause someone was in a bad fix?"

Of course, she had. She'd helped Jax steal food. Griffin patch a knife wound. Helped herself stay alive in a place where people who should've taken care of her treated her like a beast of burden. Help always had a price and a motive.

"Helpin' folks'll get you gutted when you ain't lookin'. That's gospel," she said. "Only soul you can trust on this trail is the one wearin' your boots. Learn that quick, or get buried slow."

"Well, that sure as hell ain't how I was raised." He gestured back toward the east. "Back at the orphanage, fella named Luke ran the place. He taught us we was all we had in this world. That when one boy was sick, the others brought him water. When one was struggling with his letters, another would help him."

He's an orphan.

She stared at him, searching his face for some sign of the hardness, the cunning, the deep, abiding suspicion that came as a birthright of every orphan she had ever known. She saw *none* of them. It made her think he was telling the truth—that an orphanage where they gave you community and friendship existed—but that had to be a fantasy.

Orphanages offered cold floors and thin blankets, gruel for breakfast, and callous hands. You learned to fight for your scrap of bread and trust *no one* because the bigger kid would steal your shoes and the matron would work you until you dropped.

That was the truth.

A dozen confessions rose to her lips. *Me too. I was at one. It wasn't like yours.* The words clamored to get out, to forge a connection based on this one, shocking piece of common ground.

She choked them back.

To tell him would be to open a door. And through that door, more questions would come. *Which orphanage? Where? Who did you know there?* And the answers to those questions led to Jax. To The Thorns. To a life she was desperately trying to bury. Sharing a secret meant giving them a loaded gun. You had to trust them not to pull the trigger, and June Crow trusted *no one*.

Cole watched her with a frustrated look on his face, but she gave him nothing.

She turned her gaze forward, toward the sluggish brown river, her hands tightening on the reins. It was better this way. Let him be frustrated and think she was heartless and cold. She'd always pay such a small price to save her life.

"The line's crawlin' again," she said.

She flicked the reins, and the heavy wagon lurched forward with a groan, leaving him standing alone in the mud. She kept her eyes fixed ahead, chewing her lip until it was raw.

Chapter Seven

Late May 1852, (Approx. 2–3 weeks into the journey)

Along the Platter River valley, Nebraska

The sun bled out across the horizon, painting the sky in bruised shades of purple and orange. The day's oppressive heat relented and withdrew into an evening chill that carried the scent of dry grass. Around Cole, the wagon train shaped a tight circle, within which families made campfires and cooked.

Conversations murmured, burning wood crackled, tin plates being washed clattered, and the steers settling for the night lowed. The noise showed the community Luke had preached about and Travers had demanded. Yet, as Cole sat on a log, nursing a cup of lukewarm coffee, a profound sense of isolation settled over him.

Sure, he worked with the group, but he moved like a gear grinding against its fellows. June behaved as if he'd handed her a live scorpion whenever he tried to talk to her. Who had hurt her so badly that she saw danger in a helping hand?

"Aaaaaaaghhhh!"

A woman's scream came from the cluster of wagons belonging to the Marlowes and the widowed sisters.

Every head in the camp snapped up. Conversations died mid-sentence. Men reached for the rifles that always lurked close at hand. Cole jumped to his feet, his coffee cup tumbling to the ground, and ran.

Other men moved with him. Joe Marlow sprinted from where he'd been talking to Travers, and Silas and Elias loped towards the sound from the other side of the fire Cole had had to share with them.

Cole arrived to find Pearl, the younger of the two widowed sisters, pressing her back against a wagon field. Her face had turned ashen, one hand covering her mouth. Her older brother, Gideon Calder, stood frozen a few feet away, looking pale and useless.

The scream's cause coiled in the dirt not three feet from Pearl. A rattlesnake as thick as a man's forearm, its diamond-patterned back blending with the dusky ground. Its tail buzzed. It raised its head, its black tongue flicking.

Silas rushed past Cole, drawing a heavy skinning knife from his belt.

Cole froze and watched. His experience from Slade's way— the barn spiders and occasional garter snake he'd dealt with— had nothing to offer him here. This was a *rattlesnake*. One bite, and he'd be a goner.

Silas feinted with his left hand, and the snake struck, its fangs hitting empty air. In that split second of recovery, Silas lunged. His arm blurred. The knife flashed. The rattling stopped. The snake's severed head fell to the dust, its body still writhing in a grotesque spasm. Silas flicked the head away with his boot, then nudged the twitching body with his knife.

Pearl let out a shuddering sob and sank to the ground. Her sister, Savannah, rushed to her side, murmuring reassurances.

Wiping his knife clean on his pants and sheathing it, Silas glanced over at Cole.

Cole prepared for a sneer and a condescending remark about his own hesitation.

"You grab one by the tail, they'll twist 'round and sink them fangs 'fore you can spit." Silas gestured with his chin toward the dead snake. "Best way's to get its eye, let it strike, then take the head clean off. Quick's the trick."

Cole blinked. "Thanks…"

So far, all Silas ever told him carried Elias' brand of casual cruelty. Now, he'd given him a piece of practical knowledge that could save his life. As hard as he tried, Cole just couldn't think of a reason for the sudden change.

Silas grunted, then spat a stream of tobacco juice into the dust. "Plenty folks out here fret only 'bout outlaws and injun raids."

"Ain't that a fair worry?"

"Sure is, but this, here…" Silas nudged the snake's body again. "This'll kill ya quicker. Prairie don't give a damn if you're preacher or sinner. You ain't watchin', you ain't livin'."

He gave Cole one more lingering look, then turned and walked away, melting back into the shadows beyond the firelight.

Cole helped Joe Marlowe calm the remaining onlookers and made sure Pearl was alright before heading back to his spot.

***

The camp slept.

The fires had burned down to glowing red embers. Crickets chirped, and the wind sighed. The moon offered just enough light to turn the canvas wagon tops into a herd of wraiths.

Cole had first watch.

He walked the perimeter of the camp, cradling the old Henry-style lever-action rifle Travers had given him. Responsibility dwelled on his shoulders, a weight he found both heavy and welcome. He guarded a flock of fifty souls. The clear-cut duty chased away, at least for a moment, the confusing gray areas of his relationship with June and his friction with Elias and Silas.

The vacuum of the night overwhelmed him.

At Slade's Way, fences and buildings contained the dark. Here, it unfurled into infinity. It rolled on forever in every direction in a black sea. A billion stars stared at him from above, pressing into him until he shrank to the size of a mouse.

He strained his ears for anything unusual.

Over the last few weeks, he'd become accustomed to mice and other critters rustling in the grass while the wagons' riggings hissed under the wind. Steer chewing, and the occasional stamp and snort of a horse.

CRUNCH!

The crack sounded heavier than the scuttling of a prairie dog or the slow thread of a wandering cow. It came from the darkness just beyond the ring of firelight.

Cole froze, his thumb finding the hammer of his rifle, and peered into the gloom.

There. A flicker of movement. A shape slipping between two of the outer wagons. It sculked low and avoided the light with intelligence beyond any animal.

Raiders? A scout?

Cole knew his duty. Wake up Travers and raise the alarm. Only, what if it *was* just a trick of the moonlight or a clever animal? He'd be the laughing stock of the camp if he made a fuss about a coyote. Elias' sneer and his accusations of Cole being a jumpy greenhorn would prove true.

I have to be sure.

Cole left the immediate perimeter of the camp, moving as silently as he could. He circled around the wagons, keeping them between himself and where he'd seen the shadow, trying to cut it off. Reaching the spot where he'd thought it had been—a gap between the Marlowes' wagon and one of the supply haulers—he found only the prairie stretching out into the distance.

Did I really imagine it?

No. A prickle on the back of his neck assured Cole someone watched him.

He crouched low, his rifle at the ready, and scanned the darkness. The figure appeared again, already a hundred yards out, fleeing into a shallow ravine. Whoever it was, they were fast, and they knew the land.

Cole sighed.

He had to report it. Whether they mocked him for it or not, he had a duty, and he *would* see it through. No point in waking up Travers for this, however. The man had too many things to think about during the day for Cole to interrupt his sleep over an intruder that'd already escaped.

No, he would have to wake... Elias and Silas.

***

Cole found them wrapped in their bedrolls. He nudged Silas's shoulder first. The man woke up instantly, his hand going to the knife at his belt before he recognized Cole.

"What is it?" Silas grumbled, sitting up.

Elias stirred beside him. "What in Sam Hill's goin' on?"

"I spotted someone out yonder," Cole said. "Just past the wagons. Moved like he knew the land."

Elias sat up and scrubbed a hand over his unshaven jaw. "Or maybe you nodded off and dreamt up a ghost. Jackrabbit scared you?"

"It was a man." Cole frowned. "He disappeared into a ravine out west of here."

Silas stood up and grabbed his rifle. He walked to the edge of the firelight and peered out into the darkness, scanning the landscape.

"Don't see nothin'." He shrugged. "Probably a coyote. Big ones out here—catch one at the right angle, might look like a man if you got city eyes."

"I know a coyote when I see one."

"City boy like you? Give me a break." Elias laughed. "Ain't no shame bein' green. Go curl up with your bedroll and let real men keep watch."

The condescending tone punched Cole in the face. A hot flush crept up his neck, burning his ears. They were dismissing him, treating him like a hysterical child. But arguing would be pointless. It would only reinforce their opinion of him. He knew what he'd seen, but he had no proof.

"Fine." Cole strapped his rifle back to his back. "Your watch."

He turned and walked away, as their low chuckles followed him, making his shoulders hunch.

I will not second-guess myself.

It *had* been a man. Their problem if they chose to think otherwise. He'd report it to Travers in the morning regardless. For now, he'd passed on his watch and could go get some sleep.

He headed back toward the supply wagon and the tent he shared with June.

More than two weeks travelling together, and the situation persisted in being awkward. Well, to him. June kept such a good poker face, he was starting to think she wasn't human. But he couldn't help it. It wasn't appropriate for a man and a woman unmarried to share a tent, and their engagement was *fake*.

He reached the wagon and stopped.

The tent Travers had loaned them to keep the charade alive slouched under the moonlight, forming a fragile bubble of privacy. Cole stood outside it and listened to June's soft breathing from within. Shallow and uneven.

She was awake.

He slowly lifted the flap. She huddled under a thin blanket, facing away from the entrance. Her body clutched a rigid posture, and her shoulders trembled. Seeing someone as fierce as her sleeping like this—well, failing to sleep, obviously— made him ache. For all that she insisted on snapping at him and rejecting any contact, her angry façade screamed the truth at him.

She was bone-achingly afraid.

The warm air inside the tent smelled of her more than usual. The intimate size of the space stabbed his lower back. Sleeping here tonight would cross the boundary and take advantage of the lie they lived together. He would give her the space she so clearly craved. The safety of solitude.

"Don't worry," he whispered. "I won't bother you."

He let the flap fall. Resting his rifle beside him, he lay down on the ground next to the tent and crossed his hands behind his back. His bedroll and blanket had remained inside, but the night was warm enough for him to avoid going back in there.

Staring up at the army of stars above, he fought the conflicting thoughts whirling in his mind.

He was responsible for a girl who saw him as an enemy, partnered with men who saw him as a fool, and guarding a camp against a threat no one else would believe existed.

I miss Slade's Way.

Chapter Eight

Late May 1852, (Approx. 2–3 weeks into the journey).

Along the Platter River valley, Nebraska

Cold air streamed over the hill, carrying the stench that reeked of emptiness and a world man had failed to tame. Jax preferred town smells. Coal smoke, whiskey, the sweat slicking a liar's palms, and the metallic tang of a coin changing hands. Those promised opportunity.

He lay prone, the rough wool of his coat scratching his chin, the brass of his spyglass chilling his eye socket. Below, nestling in a gentle curve of the land, the wagon train stirred. From this distance, it resembled a child's scattered toys, showing a collection of miniature wagons, tiny figures moving about, and a herd of steer that crawled like beetles.

He focused on a single point among it all. A figure climbing down from the driver's seat of a heavy supply wagon.

June.

Even from half a mile away, he knew the set of her shoulders and the stiff way she moved. He'd studied that posture for years. Molded it. He'd taught her to walk with her chin up and meet the world with a glare that promised violence. Now she used it against him. The disloyalty burned like a hot coal in his gut.

"We're losing time, Jax," Griffin said.

Griffin's conscience had grown as loud and inconvenient as a church bell. Even with the spyglass pressing against his eye,

Jax knew Griffin stood there with his arms crossed and a tightening around his mouth etching itself into his face.

"Shut it."

"We've been chasin' her for weeks. We're riding into open country, heading straight for Fort Kearny." Griffith sighed. "That place ain't got no sleepy sheriff, Jax. That's the army."

A heavy footstep crunched on the gravelly soil, announcing Clay, who followed Jax like a shadow and served as his fist. "You questionin' Jax?"

Jax had cultivated Clay's devotion since they were boys scrounging for scraps behind the orphanage kitchens.

"I'm callin' this as it is. We gon' get ourselves shot or hanged over a girl who clearly wants nothin' to do with us anymore," Griffin said. "She ran, Clay. Let her go."

"Running ends for her here," Clay said. "She belongs with the crew. With Jax."

"She don't *belong* to nobody!"

Jax grumbled and lowered the spyglass. The argument grew tedious and predictable. Griffin waxed his morality, and Clay defended Jax with proper zeal. For two weeks, Jax had had to sit through the same thing.

Why do I even put up with Griffith anymore?

Jax rolled onto his back and stared up at the pale sky. Mercy sat on a rock nearby, sharpening a knife on a whetstone, the rhythmic *shhhk, shhhk, shhhk* of steel on stone doing wonders to soothe Jax's frayed nerves. She watched the two men, her expression carefully neutral, but Jax spotted the keen glint in her eyes. She loved watching Griffin squirm.

Page 64

"Griffin's right about one thing." Jax frowned. "Fort Kearny's a doggone problem. presents a problem. But problems're puzzles, and I ain't never met one I couldn't crack."

"This here's a suicide march." Griffin loomed over Jax. "For what? Your busted pride?"

Clay's face contorted, his lips pulling back from his teeth. "Watch your mouth."

"Make me."

He shoved Griffin hard in the chest. Griffin stumbled back, catching himself before he fell, and responded in kind.

"Enough."

Jax's command dragged with it ice that could stop a charging bull. It sliced between them, and both men froze.

Jax sat up.

Running his hand through his dark hair, he cuffed them with a predator's stare. Letting the silence stretch, he forced them to stand there in their half-finished fight and fret the gathering storm of his temper.

He'd learned that from his father.

The silence before the blow always terrified more than the blow itself. His father had lived as a petty criminal, a drunkard, and a failure. But the man had excelled in the application of torment. It was the only useful thing the man had ever given him.

"You boys actin' like this is some Sunday picnic." Jax tilted his head. "We're the Thorns. Ain't a crew west o' the river got our name feared like ours."

He brushed the dust from his coat and circled them like a wolf inspecting his pack.

"Let me lay it out plain for ya, Griffin, since your bleeding heart seems to have addled your brain." He stopped in front of him, close enough to see the sweat on Griffin's brow. "June ain't just some girl. She's a walkin', talkin' map o' every outlaw trick we ever pulled. She knows every hidey-hole, every fence that bought our goods, every sheriff that'd string us up."

"I know, but—"

"She knows about that deputy in Benton. Knows he's lyin' dead with one of *my* slugs in his chest!"

He let that sink in. The air grew heavy. Even Clay's expression shifted at the mention of it.

"Picture it. Our June, all scared an' lonesome, stompin' right up to that army post." His voice dropped to a whisper. "Spillin' every tale she got, tradin' it fer a pardon an' a bounty. Rope round our necks soon as she opens that purty mouth."

Griffin looked down.

Jax grabbed his cheeks and forced his head up. "You listenin' to me?"

"I am."

"She's a threat." Jax clenched. "Say it with me."

"I—"

"Now."

"She's a threat."

Jax pressed their foreheads together. "What do we do with threats?"

"She's one of us too."

Jax grabbed the back of Griffin's head with his other hand. "I asked you a question."

"We… we handle threats."

"Good." Jax patted Griffin's temple. "I ain't sayin' we gon' kill her, but we need to do somethin' about her."

"Alright."

Jax walked back to his vantage point and picked up his spyglass. "Don't worry too much about it, Griffin. She belongs to *me*. I ain't gon' damage her much."

Clay nodded, and Jax knew the simple logic of ownership would make sense to his simple mind. Griffin flinched, the possessiveness of the statement likely galling his softer nature. Still, Jax never could bring himself to resent Griffin's inherent kindness. Not fully. He'd tried to stamp it out, of course, and would keep doing so, but he never held it against Griffin. Mercy kept sharpening her knife.

"I made her." Jax raised the spyglass back to his eye, the camp swimming into focus again. "I made all of you. Did you forget that?"

Griffin exhaled. "No."

"She was nothin' but a scared, scrappy rat when I found her. I showed her how to bite. Taught her to be *somebody*. She owes me that. Isn't that right, Griffin?"

"It is."

"So, does she have the right to walk away after I invested in her so much?"

"No."

The orphanage had been a hopeless place where the weak were culled and the strong learned cruelty. He recalled the gnawing emptiness in his belly, the cold that settled deep in your bones, the casual fists of the older boys, and the matrons' weary shrugs. *Jax* had gathered them up and forged that collection of broken toys into a family. *His* family.

And she thinks she can break us apart?

"The crew is off-balance without her." He clenched the spyglass. "It functions poorly. The parts fail to fit."

Griffin served as the thinker who planned all the details of a heist. Clay provided the muscle. Mercy was more ruthless than any of them. Jax ruled as the head that drove them all. June acted as the scout, the one who could slip in and out of places unnoticed. Without her, they'd stumble.

Through the spyglass, he watched the boy who loitered around June say something to her. She snapped a reply, her body language stiffening, her shoulders going rigid. The boy looked confused, and his mouth fell open. A twisted warmth spread through Jax's chest. Good. Let her be cruel. That showed the June he had created. But the fact that she spoke to that boy at all, that she even stood near him, ground stones in Jax's gut.

He lowered the spyglass and turned to face his pack.

"She's coming back whether she wants to or not. We'll remind her what she's good at. What it feels like to have a full belly and money in her pocket."

Griffin tried to stare at him, but dropped his gaze once Jax stared back.

"Clay, watch the camp." Jax threw him the spyglass. "I want to know everything down to when each of them takes a leak.

Mercy, get some food ready. Something cold. No fires—don't want nothin' pointin' this way."

As they moved to obey, Jax turned back to the hill's edge, lying back down in the dirt, the cold seeping into his bones.

The sun climbed higher, and the camp hummed with life. That irritating boy walked away from June and approached a group of men, leaving her alone in a world that was about to close in on her.

A hollow ache echoed in Jax's chest. He missed her sharp wit. The way she could read a mark's intentions in a single glance. The easy partnership of their early days, when it was just the five of them against the world.

I'm getting soft.

He'd always worried that he'd go down that road when he got her to return his feelings. Never in his wildest dreams would he have expected her absence to trigger weakness in him. He should've shot her the moment they'd tracked down the wagon train. Yet, here he was, planning a way to get her back.

Whatever, it's fine.

Thinking of what could've and should've been was a trap anyway. What did strength and weakness matter compared to a future in which he held June by his side forever? Of course, he'd do what he had to for that future to come to pass. Lie. Steal. Kill. Didn't matter. He'd bury as many bodies as necessary to save her from the prairie and the bleak prospect of living as some simple homesteader's wife.

She'd kick and scream all the way, and he expected nothing less. That fire and stubbornness separated her from other women, but his will would overpower hers.

E.J. WEST

See you soon, June.

Chapter Nine

Early June 1852, (Approx. 3–4 weeks into the journey)

Fort Kearny, Nebraska

Fort Kearny behaved as something other than a town. It projected an image of order into a swirling sea of unsettled lives, its sod and adobe buildings huddling together on the plains. Blue-uniformed soldiers moved through the dust-caked shuffle of the emigrants. For the first time in weeks, the muffled sounds and contained air gave June the impression of solid walls around her, yet her breath shortened inside the fort's confines.

After all, this place had far fewer escape routes than she'd like.

Even worse, they had to linger here. Lenore Marlowe and her daughter had come down with a fever and a sickness of the stomach. The fort's doctor declared it food poisoning after a brief examination. It wasn't life-threatening, but they'd have to stay put for at least a few days to let the fever break.

Even though no one complained out loud, the camp obviously disliked the news.

A delay ate into their supplies, shortened the window of good weather for crossing the mountains, and, for June, carved three days from the distance between her and Jax.

She busied herself with tasks, checking the stores in the supply wagon, mending a tear in a canvas sack, anything to keep her hands and mind occupied. Anything to stop herself from scanning the horizon, from seeing Jax's silhouette in every distant rider.

"It's good that we're waiting." Cole sounded as if he were trying to convince himself as much as her. "It's the right thing to do. The Marlowes are good people."

"A delay is a delay." She focused on re-tying a rope.

His earnest tone pierced her raw nerves like a hot poker. He lacked any comprehension of the stakes. For him, a delay meant only a minor setback. For her, it represented a death sentence ticking closer.

He eventually walked away. The pained confusion clouding his face was another black mark on the tally of things she hated about this situation.

On the second afternoon of their wait, a Pony Express rider came to ruin June's day.

He rode in atop a fine-looking horse that foamed with sweat and trembled from a likely long run, but the man himself showed a far worse spectacle. He had a boy's face, his skin pale under a layer of grime and streaked with blood from a cut on his forehead. His clothes hung in tatters, and he swayed in the saddle as if he might fall at any moment, but his mochila still slung over his saddle.

A crowd gathered instantly.

Soldiers ran to help him, easing him from his horse as his legs buckled. Travers and some of the other men, Cole among them, moved closer. June hung back at the edge of the throng, a drumbeat throbbing against her ribs. She told herself this had nothing to do with Jax.

Riders faced attackers all the time.

They gave the man water and sat him down on a crate. The fort's commander, a man with a stern face that showed every line of his authority, knelt beside him.

"What happened, son?" the commander said.

"Outlaws." The boy coughed. "Four of 'em. Back a day's ride, near the Little Blue."

No, it's a coincidence. It has to be!

"Strange thing—they didn't want nothin'." The rider took another gulp of water. "After they roughed me up, the leader says somethin' odd, told me to remember it."

The fort commander frowned. "What was it?"

"He says, 'Some things're worth more than gold, but this ain't one of 'em.' Funny, 'cause he didn't ask for a dime."

June stopped breathing.

Some things are worth more than gold.

Jax had picked up that phrase from a book he'd stolen years ago. He thought it made him sound profound, like a philosopher king of thieves. He used it all the time, usually before doing something senselessly cruel. It was his signature, as clear as if he'd left his name carved into the boy's flesh.

They'd found her.

Her skin prickled with the phantom sensation of a hundred pairs of eyes on her, though she knew everyone focused on the rider. The fort transformed from a sanctuary into a trap. Her carefully constructed plan, her desperate flight, had collapsed.

"June? Are you alright?"

Cole stood beside her, his face etched with kindness that tightened her stomach. His dark eyes bored into her, full of questions she could never answer. His concern stung her skin like an accusation. If he knew, if anyone knew her connection to them, the group would cast her out.

"I'm fine." The words came out sharper than she'd intended.

"You look like you've seen a ghost."

I have.

"I can take care of myself." She glared at him and put every ounce of the orphanage's cruelty and the Thorns' hardness into it. "Leave me alone!"

A deep shadow of pain flashed in his eyes. She recognized the expression because she had caused it before. It gave her a bitter, hollow sensation in her chest. Better he suffer a wounded spirit than someone cut his throat.

She turned her back on him and walked away.

She found herself near the Marlowes' wagon, drawn there without conscious thought. Lily's whimpers reached her from inside, and the soothing murmur of Lenore's voice followed. Joe sat on the wagon tongue, his head in his hands, his entire posture screaming defeat.

He looked up as she approached. "She's no better. The fever won't break. The doctor says we need to keep her hydrated, but she can't keep anything down."

June looked at this good and simple man, his life completely upended by a bit of bad meat. His suffering was so pure. It had nothing to do with secrets, lies, or running from a violent past. Seeing him so helpless cracked something inside her. A sensation she had suppressed for years resurfaced.

Care for someone else.

"Quinine," she said.

Joe looked at her. "The fort's surgeon doesn't have any. He used the last of it last week."

"The sutler's store might," she said. "The private one, the one that serves the trappers. They sometimes have things the army doesn't."

She'd gleaned that piece of knowledge from years of listening to thieves and traders.

Joe shook his head. "Ain't no way he shows that to someone like me."

The impulse struck her with sudden and overwhelming force, an act of rebellion against the calculating survivor she had forced herself to be. It offered a way to do something, anything, other than sit and wait for Jax to find her. It provided a way to push back against the darkness, even in this insignificant way.

"I'll go," she said.

Joe looked at her as if seeing her for the first time. "You'd do that?"

June only nodded, unable to speak past the strange lump in her throat.

"Thank you." He reached into his pocket. "Let me give you the money—"

"Keep it." She shook her head. "I'll take care of it."

She had her own money. Stolen money, yes, but using it for this felt right. A tiny act of atonement.

As she walked away, Joe's voice followed her.

"You're a good girl, June Crow."

The words stopped her in her tracks. A good girl. No one had called her *that* before. Ever. At the orphanage, she had been a troublemaker, a thief, a survivor. With the Thorns, she had been cunning and dangerous. Jax had called her beautiful. Never *good*.

Yet, hearing the words from this decent man touched a part of her soul she thought had died long ago.

She glimpsed a different June, imagining a woman she might have become in a different world. A person she could, perhaps, still become. If she lived that long. The thought gave her a flicker of something she had long since buried.

A small ember of hope.

***

Cole watched her walk away, a tight knot coiling in his gut, its strands woven from his churning thoughts and gnawing unease. Her reaction to the news about the crew went beyond simple alarm.

It was the kind of dread that came with recognition.

He was as sure of this as he was that the sun rose in the east. However, her refusal to confide in him left him with his hands tied. He could do little to protect her if he had no idea what he was protecting her from.

He turned his attention back to the crowd, which began dispersing.

The fort's commander promised to send a patrol out to scout the area, but the damage had already spread. A new layer of tension settled over the camp's already unsettled mood. Now, every shadow would hold a potential threat, every night watch would be twice as tense.

Cole went back to his work.

An hour later, as Cole helped Travers fix a wagon wheel, he spotted a man walking toward their encampment.

He walked with an easy gait out of place with the fort's strained atmosphere.

Cole paused in his work, wiping sweat from his brow with the back of his hand. The man sent goosebumps up his spine, just like when one of the younger boys prepared to do something stupid back at Slade's Way.

Something about this man rubbed him the wrong way.

He was young, maybe a few years older than Cole, and had a lean build. He had the weather-beaten look of someone who spent most of his time outdoors, his skin tanned to the color of worn leather. His clothes looked dusty but of good quality, and a pistol with a well-cared-for wooden grip hung low on his hip. On the surface, he resembled any other trapper or scout passing through.

But his eyes drew Cole's attention.

As he drew closer, their washed-out blue color became clear. They scanned the camp with a quick, predatory intelligence that missed nothing. Then the man offered a smile. The expression showed friendliness and an easygoing manner that vanished *before* reaching those cold eyes.

It was a mask, and it hid great danger behind it.

The man veered directly for Travers, and Cole fought the urge to step in his path and start a fight. As sure as Cole was of his assessment of the man, he couldn't just attack him without cause. It'd get him thrown off the wagon train faster than he could blink.

The man stopped a respectful distance from Boone and removed his hat. "Afternoon. If you don't mind me sayin', you run your outfit well."

Travers stared at the wheel. "I reckon I do."

"Name's Axel." The man smiled. "I hoped you might have room for one more. I'm headed for the Oregon territory. Got my own horse and kit, and I can pay my way."

Travers straightened and gave Axel a long look. "Appreciate the offer, but we have a full party."

"Sorry to hear that." The man inclined his head and left.

As Axel left the edge of the camp, Elias came running.

"Travers!" Elias skidded to a halt in front of the wagon. "We got a problem!"

"What is it?" Travers said.

"I can't find Silas anywhere."

Chapter Ten

Early June 1852, (Approx. 3–4 weeks into the journey)

Fort Kearny, Nebraska

Their wagons circled up ahead, the canvas tops glowing like fragile beacons against the dusk, offering only a flimsy illusion of security. Then her eyes found Cole. He stood near the supply wagon, his back to her, talking to Travers. He turned, as if some current in the air had signaled her approach, and his eyes met hers from fifty yards away. The earnest line of his brow and the open set of his mouth made her stomach clench.

He walked toward her, his long-legged stride eating up the distance between them.

Don't. Just leave me alone. Go back to your mules and your naive ideas about the world.

She knew he wouldn't, of course. One thing she'd learned about Cole Slade was that he always sought to mend things. Fix what lay broken. Aid anyone in front of him. Now, he fixed on her as if she were a snapped axle he meant to repair.

He reached her just as she arrived at the edge of their camp, his presence casting a large shadow over her, blocking the afternoon sun.

"Where were you?" He glanced toward the Marlowe's wagon. "Are Lenore and Lily...?"

"The fever hasn't broken." She held up the bottle. "This might help."

"That's good." The genuine compassion in his voice grated against her nerves like sand in her eye. "I'm glad you finally—"

"Stop." She sidestepped him. "Don't read more into it than what's there."

She wanted only to deliver the medicine and find a dark corner to crawl into, but he put a hand on her arm to stop her.

"Be mad at me all you want, but this is a good thing."

"Can I go?"

"There's something else." His expression changed, his brief smile vanishing to a tautness she would never expect to see on his face. "When you left... a man came into camp."

An icy current shot up from the soles of her feet, turning her blood to ice water. She stared at him, her throat closing up until she could barely draw breath.

She gulped. "What man...?"

Cole glanced back over his shoulder, toward the center of the camp where Travers now talked to a small group of men. She followed his glance.

The world stopped.

Literally. For an eternal second, the sounds of the fort—the wind, the distant hammer, the lowing of cattle—vanished from her ears. The light warped, the edges of her vision blurring into a gray tunnel. Her nightmare waited at the center of that tunnel. He stood with a relaxed posture, his hat pushed back on his head, listening intently to Travers. Wore clean clothes. Looked respectable, even.

She knew better.

It was all a performance. The wolf in sheep's clothing had already sunk his teeth into the heart of June's escape plan, and Travers and the others had no idea.

Jax.

She dragged a breath through her teeth. Her eyes darted past him, counting wagons, noting how far the Marlowes' canvas stretched, where Boone stood, where Elias leaned on his rifle. If she screamed now, if she ran—no, too many ways for him to catch her. The quinine bottle weighed down her hand like a rock. She flexed her fingers tight around its neck until they burned. A bead of sweat slid behind her ear, and she wanted to fling it off like a bug crawling on skin.

The quinine bottle slipped from her numb fingers, and she used every ounce of her will to snatch it from the air before it shattered on the hard-packed earth. The near-disaster sent a jolt of adrenaline through her, preventing her legs from giving out. She stared, frozen, her heart a wild bird battering itself against the cage of her ribs.

"That's him." Cole frowned beside her. "Calls himself Axel. He wanted to join the train. June, there's something wrong with him. I can feel it. He's a threat."

She swallowed hard, but the taste of bile stuck to her throat. Her legs twitched to bolt for the tree line, drag Joe's family with her, and vanish before that smirk landed again. She knew better. Men like Jax cut off exits before you smelled the smoke. She pictured him walking tent to tent tonight, meeting eyes, feeding lies. He could fool them all before dawn.

An uncontrollable tremor started deep inside her. She wrapped her arms around her stomach, trying to physically hold herself together, trying to stop from breaking apart right there in the dust.

Cole's instincts had rung like a death knell, and he had no idea.

"June?" He put his hand on her shoulder. "What's wrong?"

Cole's face blurred in front of her. She blinked, and his frown sharpened again. He squeezed her shoulder, heat seeping through her dress sleeve, a living anchor that made her knees lock in place. He said her name again, softer, his breath brushing her temple. June fought the urge to bury her face against his chest and vanish behind him like a frightened child.

The human contact, the ice in her veins, the absolute jolt of seeing Jax standing there so calmly—it combined to break something in her. A crack appeared in the iron wall of her self-control, and before she could stop it, the truth, or a sliver of it, spilled out.

"I know him," she whispered.

Cole's grip on her shoulder tightened. "What? Who is he?"

She quivered. "Tell me Travers turned him down."

"He did, but—"

"No, Cole. No buts. Tell me Travers turned him down."

"Silas is missing."

The announcement landed like a hammer blow, and June watched the final pieces of Jax's terrible plan fall into place. Silas vanishes. A spot on the train opens up. And a capable, willing stranger named Axel happens to be standing right there. The design revealed its simple elegance and breathtaking cruelty. Jax had created his own way in, and Silas had paid the price. The cold certainty of it settled in her soul.

Silas lay dead in a ditch somewhere.

Cole leaned closer. "June, who *is* he? Did he hurt you?"

She jerked back half a step. Her boot heel caught a rut in the dirt and held her still. "Don't, Cole."

He stepped forward again. "Tell me. Let me go to Travers. We can run him off."

"You can't." She stared at the dust on his boots. "You can't fix this."

"Try me." His hand caught her wrist. "What did he do?"

June's voice cracked. "Everything."

She watched, as if from a great distance, as Travers' face hardened, and gathered men looked at each other, their faces slackening and their eyes widening. She gritted her teeth as Travers' weary gaze fell upon Jax. The wagon master obviously disliked him—she read it in the set of his jaw—but she knew he cared about the success of the wagon train above all. He had to get it to Oregon and now lacked a hand.

"Alright, Axel," Travers' voice boomed across the camp and sealed her fate. "You said you were looking for work. The spot's open. You're hired."

No!

She stood frozen, a statue carved from ice. Jax tipped his hat to Travers with a gracious smile. Then, as if her stare had physically pulled at him from across the camp, he turned his head. His eyes found hers.

The polite mask he wore for the others dissolved, and for a split second, the real Jax glared back at her. He burned with a possessive heat and the cold light of triumph. The absolute certainty of his ownership of her. He smirked. A tiny, almost imperceptible, lift at the corner of his mouth, but it delivered a message with the force of a branding iron.

'You belong to me,' it said. *'There's nowhere on this earth you can run where I will not find you.'*

A broken sound escaped her lips. "You can't... you can't ever escape..."

"What did you say?"

Cole's question snapped her from her trance. The survival instinct, the one life had beaten into her since childhood, roared back to life. She had made a terrible mistake. She had let Cole see the chinks in her armor. Admitted she knew Jax. She had to build the wall back up, now, before he could ask any more questions.

She pulled her arm from his grasp and turned to face him, forcing her features into a mask of cold annoyance while her heart tried to claw its way out of her chest.

"I said nothing."

"You said you know him." Cole's dark eyes narrowed, searching her face. "June, who is he? If he's a threat, we have to tell Boone."

"Tell him what?" she hissed. "That your new fiancée has a 'feeling' about the man he just hired? That I 'know' him from somewhere? What do you think he'll do, Cole? He'll ask questions. Questions I can't answer. It will only make things worse."

A conflict played across his features, his ingrained need to act warring with the stark logic of her words. He obviously wanted to do the right thing, but possessed enough sense to see that a vague accusation from a strange, silent girl would achieve nothing.

"If he's dangerous…"

"Then the last thing you should do is challenge him." She gulped. "You have no idea what he's capable of. Just drop it."

"I can't do nothing."

"Let me handle it."

"How?"

She shook the quinine bottle in front of him. "I have to give this to Joe."

The excuse provided the perfect shield. The act of unimpeachable goodness allowed her to flee. She turned her back on him before he could ask another question and see the tremors still shaking her to her core.

She walked toward the Marlowes' wagon on wooden legs, her every sense screaming. Jax was in the camp. He would sleep near them, eat at the same fire, walk the same watch. The monster from her past had become part of her present, and he had just been handed a key to her future.

The thin flicker of warmth she had cultivated—a warmth born from a kind man's words and a simple act of charity—vanished, snuffed out as completely as a candle in a hurricane. Only the trap remained. And she stood inside it, locked in with the predator.

Chapter Eleven

Late June 1852

Approaching Chimney Rock, Nebraska

Anger arrived first.

It coiled in her gut like a wild animal pacing in too small a cage. For the week since Fort Kearny, since the man calling himself 'Axel' had smiled his snake's smile and taken Silas's place, wrath had kept her company every second of every day.

Not that she would complain. She'd rather be mad than afraid.

Yet, dread crept through her like damp that threatened to rust her soul, paralyze her limbs, and steal the air from her lungs. Rage, at least, burned and kept her warm in the dark moments of the night, when her mind veered to the images of Jax dragging her away.

She hated him.

She despised the way he moved, with a predator's lazy grace that mocked the honest exhaustion in the other men's bones. The fake name he'd chosen insulted her and poisoned the air. Most of all, she loathed the way he'd fooled the others. They saw a capable hand, a quiet man who did his work without complaint.

Only June caught the cold calculation in his eyes when he thought no one was looking. The ghost of Silas McCrae in the empty space Jax now occupied.

Watching Cole hurt her the most.

Cole noticed only what stood in front of him and took it at face value. He'd had a bad feeling, yes, but Jax was a master chameleon. He'd done nothing overtly wrong, nothing to confirm Cole's initial suspicion. Now, Cole treated him with a reserved civility, the way a good man treated anyone who hadn't given him a reason not to.

The sight of it made June's teeth ache.

She drove the supply wagon with a rigid posture, clenching the reins. Every day, she had to pretend to be the quiet fiancée, and the role chafed like burlap against raw skin. The Marlowe family glanced at her with pity, and Savannah and Pearl always smiled at her softheartedly.

If they knew the truth—that they had a wolf in their flock, and the alpha who'd raised her now walked among them—they would have cast her out into the wilderness without a second thought.

Maybe I should tell Cole.

The thought kept tormenting her. She would play it out in her mind as the wagon wheels groaned their monotonous song. She'd pull him aside, her heart hammering, and the words would spill out. 'His name is Jax Rae. He's the leader of The Thorns. He killed Silas to get on this train. He's hunting me.'

Then what?

She could picture the look on Cole's face. The honest features would close. The kindness in his dark eyes would curdle into suspicion. Then revulsion. He kept talking about this Luke Slade and his inviolable moral code.

How could a man like that ever understand a girl like her?

One who had stood by while Jax did terrible things. Whose soul was a patchwork of compromises and sins she'd committed in the name of survival. Cole would see only a monster. He would look at her the way the matrons at the orphanage had—as something broken, dirty, and dangerous.

She feared that look far more than she feared Jax. So, she stayed silent.

***

Today, the landscape had changed. The endless plains gave way to rock formations. They ambled past Chimney Rock, a bizarre finger of clay and sandstone pointing a silent accusation at the sky.

"Well now, ain't that a sight?" Cole reined in his horse to ride beside her wagon. "Somethin' to tell the folks back home about, I reckon."

His awe pierced a tiny hole in her armor. He looked at the world with the eyes of a boy who'd lived in a yard all his life and now looked upon the ocean for the first time. For him, this trail was a grand adventure. It brought a bit of light to her desperate flight.

"It's just a pile of rock, Cole."

Why would I say that? What is wrong with me?

His smile faltered. "Reckon so. Still, I ain't never laid eyes on its like. Back in the Way, the tallest thing we got is the church steeple. This... this'll make a man feel plumb small."

"We *are* small," she muttered.

She peeked past him, across the circled wagons. Jax— *Axel*—tightened a cinch on his saddle, facing away from them. As if sensing her look, he glanced over his shoulder. His eyes met hers for a fraction of a second before sliding to Cole. A faint imperceptible sneer touched his lips.

One that said: *This is what you've chosen? This soft-hearted, wide-eyed fool?*

The silent message solidified a decision that had been hardening in her mind for days. She couldn't live like this, waiting for the axe to fall. The uncertainty tainted blood, making her paranoid and weak.

She had to face him.

***

The opportunity came that afternoon.

Travers guided them to a spot where a small band of Shoshone had made camp. Travers exchanged guns and iron skillets for jerky, fresh advice on the trail ahead, and an agreement to share the campsite for the day and night. The wagon train relaxed for the first time in a week. Children played near the river, women visited between wagons, and men gathered to talk and smoke.

She watched Jax.

He took no interest in the Shoshone, instead choosing to clean his rifle at the far edge of the camp, near a copse of willows that bordered a shallow stream. She knew what he was doing. He'd separated himself deliberately, creating a space for a private meeting.

He was waiting for her.

She gulped. This was foolish. But what was the alternative? To wait for him to make his move? Let *him* pick the time and place when she was at her most vulnerable?

No.

She had run from him, but she wouldn't cower.

Taking a deep breath, she set down the water bucket she'd been carrying and glanced at the center of the camp. Cole was laughing at something little Lily Marlowe had said. He looked so carefree, so completely at home in this world of simple decency—a world she was about to betray simply by walking away from it.

She turned her back on the firelight and the laughter and made her way to Jax.

***

Patience was a virtue his father had never possessed, which was precisely *why* Jax had cultivated it into a weapon. He sat with his back against a willow, the setting sun warming the polished stock of his rifle. Cleaning it with a methodical rhythm, he let the scent of gun oil calm him down.

The process of order, precision, and careful maintenance of a tool designed for a single purpose relaxed him as he listened to the sounds of the camp behind him. The murmur of voices, the alien chatter of the Shoshone, and the distant laughter of children.

Cattle.

He pitied them. They measured their lives in crops and miles. Births and marriages. They clung to their Bibles and their flimsy sense of community, believing it made them strong. They had no idea what *real* strength was.

He'd been watching them all.

Travers could be a problem. A savvy and hard man, and he missed little, but he was also practical. He'd put the needs of the wagon train above all, and Jax could use that. Elias was a blowhard, a dog whose bark was worse than his bite. Jax could use his pride to easily manipulate him.

Then there was Cole Slade.

Jax ran an oiled cloth down the rifle's barrel and smiled. He had taken the boy's measure within an hour of joining the train. Honor. Duty. Kindness. Every action testified to the weakness that his caretaker had drilled into him. Instead of realizing that he'd found a magnificent predator in June, the boy treated her as a wounded bird.

Jax found it insulting.

And June... She'd been watching him all day, her right brow doing that little twitch that meant she jigged between terror and fury. Good. He wanted her off balance. The more easily he could rattle her, the smoother her return to the Thorns would go. With far fewer casualties, too. Not that he cared whether any of these people lived or died, but they had given her a place among them.

He could respect that.

Boots crunched against the gravelly earth of the streambed, and Jax focused on his work, drawing out the moment so she would have to speak and cede the first piece of ground.

"Jax," she said with animosity she could barely hold in check.

He finished wiping down the barrel, then slowly reassembled the rifle. Only then did he lift his head, his eyes meeting hers. She stood ten feet away with her arms crossed, but her hands trembled.

"It's Axel now," he smiled. "A new name for a new man. Got a cleaner ring to it, don't it?"

"What's your game here?"

He set the rifle aside and rose to his feet, brushing the dust off his pants. He was taller than her, and he used it, taking a slow step forward. "That ain't no way to speak to a familiar face. I crossed half this godforsaken country lookin' for you."

"That trail went cold a long time ago."

"Did it?" He pushed his way into her personal space. "Thornbushes have got to stick together, June. Or have you forgotten what keeps you from gettin' trampled?"

"You put men in the ground."

"This world ain't for the gentle, June. It's for the wolves, not the sheep. A lesson I thought you'd learned at my knee." He cupped her jaw, stroking her cheek with his thumb. "Yet, that's all dust now. Clay, Mercy, Griffin... they're trail markers in the past. I'm lookin' to start clean. With you."

She slapped his arm away. "You're a liar."

"Am I?" He let his expression soften with feigned hurt. "I saw you light out. Knew you had a hankerin' for somethin' else. So I cut my own ties. I'm here to claim what's mine, June. Start over, right and proper. Just us. We can build a stake in Oregon. A real one."

She stared at him with her eyes narrowed.

He knew she was searching for the truth, and he let her. He'd built the lie carefully. It was plausible enough to plant a seed of doubt, and doubt was all he needed to begin. Her resolve wavered, and he reached out for her cheek again.

She stepped back toward the stream. "Don't touch me."

"This about that farm boy?" Jax followed her. "He's milk-fed, June. Sooner or later, his kind gets you planted in the dirt. You belong with a man who knows the teeth of this world. A man who knows *you*."

"Leave him out of this."

Jax grabbed her lower back and pulled her toward him. "You want to be with him? Over me?"

"Let go of me."

He put his other hand behind her head and was about to pull her forward into a kiss when her frowning face and clenched fists registered in his mind. No, no, he was going too fast. If he forced a kiss on her now, she'd only resent him. Plus, others could be watching.

No. He had to remind her who she was first.

"Talk is cheap." He gestured with his chin toward the Shoshone camp. "Let me show you *why* we belong together."

Her eyes widened. "What?"

"That guide traded rifles to them, Shoshone. Good ones." Jax let go of her and stepped back. "They'll have furs and other goods. They're sittin' fat and lazy. Be as easy as breathin'. A little night work."

"No..."

"You rustle up some trouble and make 'em look your way. I'll lighten their load. You remember the feel of it, don't you, June? That fire in your blood. The two of us, movin' like ghosts while the whole world sleeps."

She stared at him, and he understood. Her doomed attempt to change ran far deeper than he'd thought. The boy, the camp, this idiotic journey... they had infected her.

"No." She crossed her arms. "I ain't that girl no more. I'd sooner be with a man like him—a man who gives—rather than a man who only knows how to take."

What?

She was choosing the boy? *Weakness?* She really wanted to throw away all they had just to gain the very things he'd saved her from?

"Were you *givin'* all them years, June?" His voice slid like silk over a razor's edge. "When we cracked that merchant's strongbox in St. Joe? When we relieved that fat sodbuster of his carriage near Independence? You didn't seem to mind takin' then."

"I—"

"Your belly was full, and your purse was heavy. Don't you stand there and preach Sunday sermons at me. You wore that life like a glove for years. Only difference now is you're pretendin' it chafes."

He saw the barb hit home. The color drained from her face, her self-righteous anger collapsing into shame and confusion. He had reminded her that she could not escape what they had been, what they had done together.

He turned and walked back toward his rifle without another word.

Let her chew on that. Let her remember that her hands were just as dirty as his. He was patient. He had all the time in the world. Sooner or later, she would remember that a wolf could never truly pretend to be a sheep.

Chapter Twelve

Late June 1852

Just past Chimney Rock

Cole sat by the fire, its shallow heat hopping on his skin as his stomach filled with cold stones. Around him, the company sank into its night-rhythm. The low murmur of talk, the clatter of a pot being scrubbed, the soft nicker of a horse—all the sounds of camp pricked Cole's ears.

He had watched June walk away from the wagon with her back ramrod straight until the shadows near the stream where Axel—a name that tasted like alkali dust in Cole's mouth—had been loitering.

Cole counted it out. Twelve minutes. When she returned to the firelight, she'd gone paler than a sheet, her hands tremoring. She'd avoided Cole's eye, fussing with a water bucket as if the fate of the whole outfit depended on her filling it to the brim.

He wanted to go to her, to ask what had happened, and break through that fence she kept around herself. But he'd held fast.

Luke would've told him: *A man of good breeding don't pry, Cole. You offer a hand, you offer your protection, but you don't demand a soul's private reckonings.*

He'd always believed Luke's wisdom without question, but the longer he stayed on the trail, the more he saw that they belonged to a different world. It was a fine principle for a civilized town and the ordered world of Slade's Way. Out here, under a sky so vast it could swallow a man whole, he wasn't so sure.

Out here, secrets carried loaded pistols.

Cole poked the fire with a stick, sending a shower of orange sparks into the heavy dark. He was her fiancé. A lie, yes, but one that carried responsibility. He'd put himself in this yoke. He'd offered the shield of his name, and in doing so, he had taken on her troubles whether he'd wanted to or not.

He was failing.

Standing by, honoring a promise of distance she'd never asked for, while she wrestled a ghost invisible to him.

His thoughts tangled into a knot of rope as he replayed every run-in with Axel. The man's easy smile that never touched his eyes. The way he moved with a coiled stillness that spoke of violence kept on a short leash. His arrival, convenient as rain in a drought, just as Silas McCrae had vanished. Too many coincidences.

But a gut feeling wasn't proof. You couldn't send a man to the hangman on suspicion.

"Slade."

Cole looked up. Travers stood over him, frowning, and Elias smirked beside him. Cole's shoulders tightened. Whatever this was, it was bad medicine.

He got to his feet. "Sir."

"We got trouble." Travers clicked his tongue. "Pearl Calder. She's come up shy a locket."

Elias' smirk deepened. "Not just any trinket. Gold, with pearls set in it. Fetch a pretty penny, I'd wager."

"What's that got to do with me?"

"Funny thing, how pockets start gettin' light right when *you* join the company." Elias's chin jutted out. "And right after you start palaverin' with those savages."

Cole's ears rang as if a mule had kicked him.

Him, a thief? Branded a common pilferer after he grew up with Luke Slade's unbending measure of a man? The injustice of it fouled his lungs so much that, for a second, he couldn't draw breath.

He jumped up. "You best take that back."

"Ain't nothin' to take back if—"

"That's enough, Elias." Travers scowled at him. "You ain't here to point fingers."

Elias looked down. "Sorry."

Travers turned to Cole. "You've got a good head on your shoulders. Was it the Shoshone? Give me your honest sense of it."

Cole had no idea whether Travers *meant* the question as a gesture of trust, but Cole took it as one nonetheless. It meant more to Cole than Travers could know. The trail master, the man the whole company respected, had asked Cole—the orphan and the greenhorn—for his judgment.

Cole would honor it with the truth, or, at least, as much of it as he could speak.

"I don't think so, sir. They traded square with us. Seemed honorable men to me. It don't sit right, layin' this at their feet just for bein' strangers."

"My own thinking." Travers nodded slowly. "Means the snake's in our own camp. One of us."

"That's what I reckon too."

Travers' eyes narrowed. "You see or hear anything that didn't sit right? Anyone pokin' their nose where it don't belong?"

Here it was. The time to speak the name burning a hole in his mind. *Axel.* He could lay it all out for Travers: the bad feeling, the timing, the look on June after their talk. It would be so easy.

But he couldn't.

To accuse Axel, he'd have to say *why*. He'd have to talk about June. He'd have to say, *'She knows him from before, from an orphan house in Nebraska.'* It would be a betrayal of the worst kind. One that would shatter what little trust stood between them, and drag her troubles out for the whole camp to pick over like vultures.

And for what? A hunch?

'A man's name is all he truly owns, Cole.' Luke had said. *'You don't go throwin' mud on another's without ironclad cause.'*

"No, sir." The words burned his tongue. "I haven't seen a thing. But I'll keep my eyes peeled."

Travers studied him for a long moment as if he could see right through him, down to the churn in his gut. Then, he nodded.

"You do that, Slade. Keep those eyes sharp."

"Will do, sir."

"Hah!" Elias scoffed, taking a step closer. "He's coverin' for that little spitfire he calls his intended. I saw 'em. Her and Axel, slippin' off into the dark. Don't think I didn't. Pair of grifters, the both of 'em. In on it together."

That was *it*.

The accusation against him, he could swallow. The dismissal of his judgment, he could ignore. But the insult to June—the foul suggestion she was a common thief—crossed the line. The leash on his temper snapped.

In two quick strides, he closed the distance, grabbed a fistful of Elias's shirt, and shoved him back against a wagon wheel.

"You say one more word about her," Cole snarled with a voice he never knew he could produce, "and I will knock those yellow teeth down your throat. You understand me?"

Elias's eyes went wide. "Get your hands off me, you crazy son of a—"

"I said, *do you understand me?*"

"Slade! Blackthorn! Stand down! Both of you!"

Reluctantly, Cole unclenched his fist. He released Elias's shirt and stepped back, his chest heaving. The heat of his anger was already drowning under a wave of discomfort. He'd lost his head. He'd let this man—this situation—drag him down to a place of which Luke would have been ashamed.

Cole took a deep breath. "He slung mud on June's name."

"And you were fixin' to answer it with your fists." Travers shook his head. "That's how fellas end up pushin' up daisies over nothin' on this trail. I won't have it. Not in my outfit."

Cole and Elias looked away from each other.

Travers pointed a thick finger to a spot away from the fire. "You two. Over yonder. You're gonna sort this out, and you ain't comin' back to this fire 'til you have. Don't care if it takes 'til sun up. You'll learn to pull together, or you'll die pullin' apart. It's all the same to the prairie."

Elias sullenly pushed himself off the wagon wheel, rubbing his chest. He shot Cole a look of pure hatred before stalking off to the spot Boone had indicated.

Cole took a deep breath, trying to gentle the wild beating in his chest.

"He's a fool, but he's one of our fools." Travers put a hand on Cole's chest. "You got a good heart, son. But you got a temper under it. Don't let it be the thing that gets you in a bind. Go on."

Cole nodded and made his way to the shadows where Elias waited.

The thought of talking to Elias appealed to him about as much as wrestling a cactus, but Travers had a point. Much like a chain, every link in the outfit had to hold.

He found Elias leaning against a supply barrel with his arms crossed.

"I shouldn't have laid hands on you." Cole clenched his jaw. "That was wrong."

Elias grunted, looking away. "Reckon I had it coming."

"It's still no way for men to carry on. Travers is right. We got to pull in the same direction."

"I pulled just fine with Wyatt," Elias muttered. "He was my partner. We came out here together. Then you show up, playin' the big hero with them mules, and Travers looks at you like you hung the moon. Now Wyatt's laid up in some Kansas town with his leg snapped."

The words brimmed with resentment, but Cole caught the underlying hurt. Distress. Jealousy. Elias didn't just dislike him; he felt shoved aside. For the first time, Cole saw past the sneering bully to the young man—one not so different from himself—trying to prove his worth and hold his place.

"I didn't ask for his place on the line," Cole said quietly. "I was just lendin' a hand. I'm sorry for your partner. Mean it. But I ain't the one who broke his leg."

"Still feels like it," Elias grumbled.

"Look, I ain't tryin' to crowd you." Cole stepped closer. "Just tryin' to get to Oregon country and stake a claim. Same as you, I reckon."

Elias hummed.

"The man who raised me... he taught a fella to take a stand for what's right. Help folks in a bind," Cole said. "That's all I was doing with them mules."

"Right." Elias glared at him. "What about right now? You were fixin' to punch my teeth out."

Cole shrugged. "You can't throw dirt on a man's intended and expect him to stand by and smile."

"You've really set a store by that girl, haven't you?" Elias tilted his head. "Even though she treats you like dirt on her boot."

Cole thought of June's spooked eyes. "She's had a hard go of it. She deserves a fella to stand up for her."

Elias looked into the distance. "That new fella, Axel..."

"What about him?"

"Don't like the cut of him." Elias spat on the ground. "Somethin' ain't right. The way he watches... like a hawk on a wire, just waitin'."

Cole exhaled. "I got the same feelin'."

Elias scrubbed a hand over his jaw. "And now Pearl's locket is gone missin'."

"We got no proof," Cole said.

"No. We don't." He looked at Cole. "Alright, Slade. You and me. We'll keep a weather eye on him. And we'll cover each other's flank. But if that girl of yours is tangled in this, I ain't makin' no promises."

"She's not." Cole frowned. "She's just scared."

Elias held out his hand. "Truce?"

Cole took it. Elias gripped his hand hard, and his skin had callouses rougher than Cole's own. They were far from friends, but Cole knew he could trust their new alliance.

It was a start.

Chapter Thirteen

Early July 1852

Approaching Fort Laramie

The rain had come after sundown, a sly hissing at first that soon turned to a devil's tattoo on the canvas world of the wagon train. The miserable rain, the kind that pierced bone-deep, settled into a man's marrow with a chill no campfire could rightly burn out.

Cole lay in his lean-to, having pulled the coarse wool of his bedroll to his chin, and listened to the prairie weep. The steady drumming on the canvas ought to have been a lullaby. Tonight, it echoed the tight-wound knot in his gut.

Sleep lay in a far-off country, and Cole lacked the trail map to get there.

His mind, skittish as a green-broke colt in a lightning storm, kept chewing on the cud of the evening. The truce he'd struck with Elias reminded him of a handshake over a fresh-dug grave. It might hold, but the ground underneath wobbled mighty hard. Still, knowing someone else saw the snake in Axel gave Cole some small measure of comfort.

After all, when you had a rattler coiling in your circle, having backup made you sleep better.

He thought of June, in her own canvas shelter just a few feet away. He'd insisted on it—two small lean-tos, side by side under the overhang of the supply wagon. A nod to propriety— both foolish and thin out here—but one Cole would never waive.

Our engagement is fake after all.

With the dark pressing in and the rain turning the good earth to a sucking mire, the rules of the states seemed a long way off. Those rules belonged to a world of fences and sheriffs, not this endless, unforgiving land where a man's only law was the iron on his hip and the strength of his convictions. Truth was, just knowing she lay nearby made his chest bone thrum more than the noise of the storm.

He knew it in his bones that she wasn't sleeping either.

He pictured her lying there, still as a stone, fearing her own ghosts. What had Axel whispered to her by that stream? What devil from her past had risen up to dog her steps all the way from Nebraska?

He rolled onto his side, the musty smell of wet canvas filling his lungs.

A steer lowed—a mournful sound swallowed by a gust of wind that made the whole shelter shudder. The Oregon Trail was taking him away from every solid thing he'd ever known. The clear lines of right and wrong Luke Slade had branded on his soul were beginning to run as the endless rain of this new life blurred them.

Helping folks was right.

That, he would forever believe. But what if helping one soul meant putting the whole flock in the path of the wolves? A man protected a woman. Simple as that. But what if that woman carried a secret that could hurt everyone?

I guess I have to figure that one on my own, Luke, don't—

SQUELCH!

The sound fought through the rain outside, the sucking of shod hooves pulling from deep mud one after another. Too heavy for deer; too deliberate for stray oxen. Someone was riding through the rain and dark. Then came the wet clink of metal—a bridle ring, maybe a spur—surrendering to the damp air.

Cole went still as a dead man, every muscle pulling taut.

He'd grown far from the greenhorn he'd been. Weeks on the trail had honed his ears to the night's rhythm, and this was a break in the song. None of their outfit's riders had any business loitering about in this weather.

This was trouble.

Cole's hand found the cold stock of the Henry rifle beside him. He slipped from his bedroll—the air raisin' gooseflesh on his arms—crept to the opening of his lean-to, and peered out. The camp's cookfire had dwindled to a few sullen red embers, giving off no light to speak of. The wagons loitered about in humped shapes, their canvas tops a ghostly gray under a sky thick with clouds.

There.

A flicker of motion past the Marlowes' wagon. A shape darker than the dark around it. Then two more.

The rule was to wake Travers.

But the memory of seeing that shadow weeks back—the one Elias and Silas had called a coyote—pricked at his pride. He'd not be laughed off as a boy crying wolf again. He had to be sure. His truce with Elias was too new for Cole to test it with a false alarm.

He slipped out.

The rain plastered his thin nightshirt to his skin in a heartbeat. He moved like a phantom, using the bulk of a wagon for cover, holding the Henry low. His lungs burned. His muscles tensed. His ears throbbed with beats that thumped faster than they ought to.

He rounded the last supply wagon, and the whole scene jumped into view.

Travers held a long-barreled Colt. Beside him, Joe Marlowe clenched his own pistol. Elias stood on Travers's other side with his own rifle in hand. They faced three figures on horseback just outside the circle, their mounts shifting restlessly.

The outlaws—'cause there wasn't no way they were anything else—hid their faces behind dark and greasy bandanas, and hats they'd drawn low. Not Shoshone. The set of their saddles was wrong, and their whole manner too bold.

"Spit it out." Travers spat on the ground. "You're trespassin'."

The rider in the center, clearly the leader, leaned on his saddle horn. "Easy now, old timer. We ain't come for your stock. We come for somethin' of ours you happened to pick up."

Cole gulped. He knew, with a sickening certainty, what they'd come for.

Before the man could say more, a soft sound came from behind Travers, and June walked up behind him. Her widened eyes fixed on the three riders. Something broke and re-formed on her face. Fear made its home there, but so did weary recognition.

She knew these men.

Fierce heat shot through Cole at the sight of her pale expression, one that scorched his veins so much it hurt. An instinct older and deeper than any lesson Luke Slade had ever taught him, and Cole knew he'd found his answer.

The riders' leader swiveled his head to look at her. "There she is. Our little stray. Time to ride, June-gal. No need for these sodbusters to get bloodied on your account."

June stiffened.

Travers spoke with a voice as flat and cold as river stone. "All you'll get from this train is a bellyful of lead. Turn your horses and drift. Now."

The leader let out a dry chuckle. "She ain't your kind, farmer. She's one of us. You hear me, June? Time to come home."

June stood frozen.

Cole had heard enough. He stepped fully clear of the wagon, raisin' his rifle so the riders could see the moonlight glint off the wet barrel.

"She's stayin' put." He aimed at the leader's head. "You want her, you come through me."

The words tumbled out before he'd rightly formed them. A promise he made to the men in the rain *and* to the trembling girl behind Travers. He didn't care that their engagement was a lie. He'd protect her as if it was real.

The rain spattered, and the horses snorted. Three outlaws faced four men of the outfit.

Then, from the corner of his eye, Cole noticed another figure stepping out from the deep shadows near the back of the camp. Axel. He held his own rifle, but joined neither line. He just stood there, on the edge of the lantern light, watching, and holding his rifle loosely with its barrel pointing at the mud.

Another piece clicked into place.

The locket. Silas goin' missin'. June's terror. Now this. A man of the trail—a man of the company—would be shoulder to shoulder with his fellows. Axel's stillness shouted louder than any gunshot.

Betrayal.

Axel was either the lowest kind of coward, or he was part of this. And Cole knew, with a gut-deep certainty that turned the rain to ice on his skin, that Axel—or whatever his real name was—was *no* coward.

He was one of them. The enemy was already inside the circle.

The standoff stretched. Cole, Travers, Joe, and Elias held their ground. The leader of the riders seemed to be doing his own calculating. He looked from Travers' steady Colt, to Joe's grim face, to Cole's raised Henry, and last of all, to Elias's unexpected steel.

They were outmanned and outgunned.

"This ain't settled." The leader pointed a gloved finger at June. "You got one day. One day to ride out and meet us. You don't, and we're comin' back. And we won't be usin' our words."

With that threat hanging in the wet air, he and his men wheeled their horses and melted back into the storm, dissolving into the blackness until only the fading squelch of hooves remained.

The men of the train lowered their weapons.

The fight had ended, for now, but the threat breathed down their necks. Travers let out a long breath and wiped a hand across his soaked face. Joe Marlowe murmured a quiet prayer. Elias stared into the darkness where the riders had vanished.

Cole walked up to June.

She tremored, and a choked sob broke from her lips. Her knees gave way, and Cole made it just in time to catch her, her hands clutching at the back of his wet shirt. His arms came around her without a thought.

He pulled her in.

She buried her face in his chest, her hot tears soaking his shirt. He held her tight, one hand on the back of her head, his rifle still clutched in the other. He glared at the darkness where the brigands had vanished before glancing at the spot Axel had taken.

The man had disappeared.

But Cole had seen him. In his mind, the enemy now had four faces, not three. He held June closer, the simple act of protecting her the only clear thought in a world that had just been torn to pieces. He didn't know who she was, not rightly. But it didn't matter. They were coming for her.

And he'd be damned to perdition before he let them have her.

Chapter Fourteen

July 5th–6th 1852

Arriving at Fort Laramie

One day.

The ultimatum swung in front of the camp like a hangman's knot, as real as the mud that sucked at Cole's boots. He moved through the camp, his mind whirring as he tried to figure out a way to protect June from those brigands.

We know nothing about them.

Therein lay the problem. Three men rode in last night, but the gang could have plenty more. They could have the newest rifles and unlimited ammo. Heck, for all Cole knew, they could have doggone *cannons*. Well, that one was a little far-fetched, but Cole *had* to think about it if he didn't want them surprising him with one.

So, how do I—

"Slade." Travers grabbed his shoulder. "Step yonder with me."

Cole nodded and followed the man behind a wagon.

"Look here, Slade. I ain't one to cast stones at a filly on the run from wolves." Travers clicked his tongue. "Lord knows I've seen my share of that brand."

Cole frowned and nodded.

"But there's a heap of reasons for outlaws to want their property back, and none of 'em are Sunday prayers. Some reasons, though, are easier for this outfit to swallow than others."

"What're you gettin' at?"

"If it's just coin she owes, we can settle that score before sundown. I got a poke put by, and the folks in this train'll chip in." Travers shook his head. "But if she's a runaway wife... well, that's a different kind of trouble. A man scorned don't quit easy. We'll be in for a hell of a fight."

Cole clenched his fists. "What do you need from me?"

"Get the truth of it. Before this day is out."

Cole nodded and walked away.

He'd given June a wide berth since the riders had gone. After her first desperate collapse against him, she'd pulled away, wrapping her usual quiet around herself again like a burial shroud. She'd gone to her tent, a lonesome figure moving through the wreckage of the storm. He'd wanted to follow, to offer... what?

Comfort? He had none to give. He had only questions, and those would be the last thing she needed.

Now, as the camp readied itself for the hardest day's ride of its lives, he saw the mark of the night's terror on every face. Women moved with bird-like speed, their eyes flitting to the horizon. Men checked their rifles, their hands tight and jerky. Even children hushed, clinging to their mothers' skirts, their games bowing to a fear they could feel even if they didn't understand it.

Cole made his way to the Marlowes' wagon first, where Joe hitched their oxen.

"Mornin', Joe," Cole said.

"Cole." Joe stared at the yoke. "A hard night."

"That it was. But mornin's broke." Cole clapped a hand on the man's shoulder. "Fort Laramie ain't far. One last hard shove, and we'll be behind its walls 'fore the moon is high. Walls and soldiers, Joe. Those riders won't get within a sniff of us there."

Joe looked at him. "It's Lenore and Lily I'm thinkin' on. That trouble last night... it ain't fit for their eyes."

"Lord willing, they won't see it again." Cole clenched the man's shoulder. "This here's a tough outfit, Joe. We faced 'em down once. We'll do it again if it comes to that. But it won't. We're gonna run. We'll run 'em ragged, 'til their horses break and their spirit with 'em. We'll do it as one."

Joe nodded and returned to hitching with more vigor. A small thing, but a start.

Cole moved on to Pearl and Savannah Calder, who packed their wagon with shaking hands. He offered a firm word and a promise of safety. Then, he spoke with the other families and played the part of the confident trail hand.

The more he said the words, the more he found himself believing them.

This was what Luke had meant by leading. It wasn't about being the strongest or the loudest. It was about being the rock in the flood, the one who stands firm so others can find their footing.

He avoided June.

Every part of him wanted to go to her and press her for the truth Travers demanded. But he couldn't. Not yet. He couldn't put her on the spot in front of the others and let them see him hounding the very girl who'd been the target.

He had to wait.

Cole also avoided Axel. *Everyone* did. Even those who hadn't seen Axel standing there like a stump during the standoff felt a coldness coming off him, which had nothing to do with the morning chill. He always had the look of a man holding a royal flush and just waiting for the last fool to put his chips in the pot.

Travers took his horse to the head of the outfit. "Wagons, ho!"

They moved out like a routed army, whips cracking like rifle shots, wheels groaning in a collective cry. Cole rode his horse alongside the train like a scout and a sheepdog both. Threats jumped at him from every corner of the hostile world. He rode hard, pushing both the animals and himself, but still unable to find the solution to June's problem.

June drove the supply wagon.

Her small body hummed with tension that struck him from fifty feet away. He wanted to ride beside her, to talk to her, but the words stuck in his craw. What could he say?

Who are they, June? Why do they want you?

It would only sound like an accusation. As if he didn't want to fight for her. No, he had to wait till they were safe.

***

The day turned into a pure-T hell of mud and sweat.

The sun burned through the fog, turning the damp to steam. Wagons lurched through muck, animals straining. They forded a shallow creek that near took a wagon and crawled through a stretch of broken country, the big wheels groaning a sorry kind of prayer. Through it all, Cole rode the line, lending a hand and shouting encouragement.

113

He blurred everywhere at once with only one thought in mind. Get them to the fort.

Axel always prowled at the edge of Cole's vision. The man rode easy, watching the others like a hawk even as he did all his duties. His calm unnerved Cole more than any show of force, because Axel had the look of a coyote that knew the rabbit had no place left to run.

As the sun began its slow bleed into the horizon, Fort Laramie rose in a smudge against the bruised sky.

They stumbled in at nightfall, in a train of exhausted and mud-caked pilgrims finding the edge of civilization. Well, somewhat of a civilization. Adobe buildings sprawling behind a low wall. Yet, the sight of uniformed soldiers, the smell of cook-fires, and the sound of men talking of everyday things brought great comfort to the murmurs of the wagon train.

Travers talked to the fort commander and got the outfit a promise of extra sentries.

Cole found an inn just inside the walls, a rough-planked building that promised a solid roof and a locked door. He paid for two rooms and led June there, letting his hand lay on the small of her back.

She limped beside him with the exhaustion of someone who'd given up the fight.

"This one's yours." Cole opened a door. "Bolt it. Don't open it for nobody but me."

She looked at him, her eyes wide and dark in the lantern light. For a second, he thought she might speak, that the dam might *finally* break. But she nodded and slipped inside, and the heavy bolt slid home.

Cole sighed and left to gather supplies. They'd need food better than hardtack and salt pork, and some of the money Luke had given him still jingled in his pocket.

***

The general store had everything from flour sacks to calico bolts to bottles of Dr. Good's Wonder Tonic. It smelled of canvas, leather, and whiskey.

As Cole waited for the storekeeper to cipher his bill, his eyes drifted to the wall behind the counter. It swarmed with notices, land claims, and army orders. Among the throng, a sheet of paper stopped the blood in his veins.

A Wanted poster.

The ink had faded, the paper yellowed and fly-specked, but the words remained clear.

WANTED FOR ROBBERY AND MURDER

THE THORNS GANG

Four drawings taunted him below. A man with a dark gaze and a cruel mouth—the one Cole knew as Axel: *Jax Rae*. A brutish-looking man: *Clay Dalton.* A woman with a hard face: *Mercy Dillon.* And the fourth... the fourth was a girl. The drawing was crude, but there was no mistaking it. The haunted eyes. The set of that small chin.

June Crow.

Cole stared at her face. June. A member of a gang wanted for robbery and *murder*. Travers had been worried she'd escaped from a husband. This was so much *worse*. A husband chased a wife out of pride and anger. These outlaws hunted June for the secrets she knew.

Cole gritted his teeth.

Her attitude to mercy. Her reluctance to aid others. The whispered conversation with Jax, and her fear. The girl he'd been protecting—the one he'd offered his name to, whose plight had stirred something fierce in him—was an outlaw.

How could I be so stupid?

***

He knocked on her door. "June. It's Cole. Open up."

The bolt scraped back, and the door creaked open. Her skin had gone pallid, but her posture remained upright. In a situation he'd have expected her to hunch and try to become a mouse, she stood tall as if she were preparing to roar and attack. The girl with the rage on that poster was right in front of him.

He stepped inside, letting the sack drop to the floorboards with a thud.

Closing the door, he pressed the wanted poster against her chest and stepped back. She unfolded the yellowed paper and held it between her fingers like a drawn blade.

He watched her face.

Saw the knowing flicker in her eyes, then the furrow of her brow. She turned the full force of her glare and gritting teeth at him, as if he were the one to blame for her criminal history.

"Don't you dare judge—"

"Tell me this paper's a lie."

She let the poster float to the ground and clenched her fists.

"We all make mistakes."

"They're wanted for murder, June. *Murder!*"

"I know." She exhaled. "That's why I lit out. It used to be just takin'. Lightenin' the load of outfits that were heavy with coin."

"So you were a thief?"

"It was wrong; I know that deep down. But it was the only way to fill our bellies."

"What happened?"

She moved her head away, still keeping her eyes closed. "The last couple scores, he put men in the ground. For nothin'. A lawman. A farmer just workin' his dirt. He... he got a taste for it. I couldn't stomach it no more. I had to run."

He glared at her. "And now they're here to drag you back, to make sure your tongue don't wag and send 'em to the hangman."

She finally looked at him. "Cole, *please*, you gotta believe me. I swear on my life, I wanted to tell you straight. I was just too scared."

"Of what?"

"This!" She breathed heavily. "Of you starin' at me just like this!"

He looked at her, this girl—this *outlaw*—and swallowed back scorching bile that had climbed his throat. He had stood up for her honor against Elias, and, now, it turned out Elias *had been right*. He had made himself her shield, and all the while, she'd been carrying this poison.

"You should've told me the damned truth," he said, "instead of lettin' me play the fool. You put every soul on this train— Joe, his wife, that little girl—square in the path of a killer. And for what? To save your own skin?"

"And what was I supposed to say?!" Tears cut paths through the grime on her cheeks. "You're always talkin' 'bout doin' right. Saint Cole Slade, with a kind word for every stray dog and hard-luck case. Everyone but me."

"Maybe I'd have found some. If I hadn't found out from a scrap of paper tacked to a wall."

"You'd have handed me over to the law." Her hair fell over her as she trembled with anger. "You'd have looked at me then the same way you're lookin' at me *now*. Like I'm dirt. Like I'm something you found on the bottom of your boot. All 'cause I did what I had to, just to stay alive."

He scowled at her.

She was a *stranger*. A part of him—the one that Luke Slade raised—knew he ought to feel something for her terror. But an avalanche of betrayal had buried that part six feet under. She'd used him. She'd let him in on a poker game he hadn't been ready to play and cleaned him out.

He picked up the poster and crumpled it, crushing her face along with the others. "I don't even know who the hell you are."

He turned and walked out, leaving her door hanging open. He went to his own room and sat on the edge of the cot, letting his rampaging heartbeat thump in his ears.

He'd wanted a test. To prove himself.

The trail had given it to him. It had thrown him a liar, a thief, and a murderer's woman for a partner.

He lay back on the thin mattress, boots and all, and stared up at the dark ceiling. He'd helped bring the outfit to the fort, but he'd never been more lost in his entire life. He hollowed, waiting for a dawn he no longer believed would bring any light.

Chapter Fifteen

July 6th, 1852

Just outside Fort Laramie

Jax lay on a low ridge, out of sight of the lookouts at Fort Laramie, the rough wool of his duster scratching at his jaw, and he waited. Usually, he lauded patience as a tool, but today, it itched the back of his neck like a dash chore.

The waiting salted a fresh wound.

His slow boil was coming to a simmer. Rage that turned a man's blood cold instead of hot and made the whole world as sharp as a razor's edge.

His plan had been a piece of art.

Slipping in as Axel, walking with the flock, learning their ways and soft spots. Giving June every chance to see the truth. Her running would come to nothing, and her new friends would break when it mattered most. He'd even given her a simple out—Clay, Griffin, and Mercy to play as night riders— so that the outfit wouldn't think ill of her.

That's what I get for having mercy.

Instead of coming to him in the dark, busted and ready to give in, she'd huddled behind that sodbuster, Slade. She might as well have spat in his face.

He lowered the looking glass.

Down below, the wagon train stirred, fixing to leave the fort's meager shadow. They scrambled like ants on a hot skillet, and Jax knew that June sat at the heart of it with her new pet.

A low growl rumbled in his chest.

He couldn't wrap his head around it. The same June he'd raised from a half-starved Nebraska pup into a predator was throwing everything they had for *this*? For a *boy* who spouted words like honor and duty. One whose strength stood on a hollow foundation of rickety morals of a world that had tossed Jax and June aside like garbage.

Cole Slade was a poison.

His straight-arrow goodness infected everyone it touched, and it'd got into June's blood. Oh, Jax saw the way the boy looked at June, with that cow-eyed gaze. As if he could smooth June's sharp edges, ease her suspicion, or curb her magnificent talent for staying alive. That son of a gun was trying to sand a hawk down into a chirping house finch.

The crunch of boots on gravel behind him broke his thoughts.

Clay, Mercy, and Griffin crested the rise. Clay stared ahead with a face of stone. Mercy looked sour, her hand resting on the hilt of her knife. Griffin gave the impression of a man who'd just swallowed a hornet.

"Jax, this is a fool's errand." Griffin stepped in front of the others. "Hitting a train this close to the fort's guns? The whole damn place is crawlin' with bluecoats. We oughta be halfway to Missouri with a fat purse, not chasin' ghosts—"

"There is no other score." Jax rose to his feet. "You've gone cloudy on the reason for this, Griffin. This ain't about plunder. It's about settlin' a debt."

"A debt?" Griffin scoffed. "She don't owe us a plugged nickel!"

Clay took a hard step toward Griffin. "You're treadin' on a rattler, Griffin."

"Enough." Jax circled Griffin like a wolf sizing up a dog. "She owes me her very breath."

"Jax—"

"I plucked her from the dirt when she was nothin'. Gave her a name. A family." He flared his nostrils. "Ain't no coin can pay for that."

"She's a grown woman, Jax, not some filly you branded," Griffin said, though the starch had gone from his voice.

"Are we chewin' this same gristle again?" Jax smiled, a cruel slash in his sun-browned face. "You in a hurry for a necktie party? I sure ain't. We don't leave loose tongues, Griffin. We cut 'em out at the root."

The finality of it shut Griffin up.

Mercy kept avoiding Jax's eye, sharpening a knife that was already keen enough to shave with. Jax knew she'd always been jealous of the attention he'd paid June. Part of her would definitely rejoice that June had fled, and another would hate him for going to these lengths to get her back.

Not that it mattered. She'd stay loyal no matter what, and Jax cared about nothing else.

"The time for skulkin' in the shadows is done," Jax said.

The announcement made breathing easier. The pretending had been wearing on him. Playing *Axel*, the quiet hand, had strained him. The time had come to shed that skin.

"That warning shot was just noise to 'em. They think that fort, their numbers... they think that gives 'em sand." Jax frowned. " It's time we learn 'em a real lesson in fear."

He turned his gaze back to the trail leading from the fort. The wagon train was crawling now, a clumsy snake of canvas and wood.

His eyes narrowed. "We're done waitin'. We ain't askin' no more. We'll be a thunderstorm, right here in the open. We will break them, and we will remind *June* what it means to cross the Thorns."

Jax swung into his saddle, the leather groaning under him. Drawing his Colt, he rode down the ridge in a mean-looking trot. He wanted the outfit to see him. He wanted them to feel that icy dread, to have a few terrible moments to ponder their mistake.

A man on a horse—Elias, the loudmouth—galloped back toward the lead, hollering a warning. The wagons slowed, the line breaking into a tangled mess.

Jax pushed his horse to a canter, the three behind him fanning out. He rode straight for the lead steer. At the last second, he swerved, pulling his horse alongside the oxen. In one swift move, he grabbed the lead ox's bridle and yanked it hard, bringing the animal to a stop. The whole train shuddered to a halt behind them.

Travers stormed up to him with his hand on his pistol. "What in the blue blazes do you think you're doin', Axel, breaking formation like that?"

"The name is Jax Rae." Jax pointed his Colt at Travers' heart. "And you're standin' in my light."

Travers' eyes widened, and he jumped under the wagon just as Jax shot.

The bullet he'd meant for the old man's chest struck his shoulder. Screams tore out from the wagons. Women cried out.

Men yelled. The beautiful chaos had begun. Jax sat tall in his saddle, letting the fear wash over them all. He savored it.

This was power.

"My name is Jax Rae!" He fired into the air. "I lead The Thorns! And I've come to collect what's mine! Send out the girl! June Crow! Do it now, and the rest of you might live to see the sun go down!"

He scanned the outfit, hunting for her, and found her by the supply wagon, next to Slade. Her face had an expression of terror that gave him deep satisfaction, but she didn't cower. She held her chin up and her back ramrod straight. She stood closer to Slade than was right, her shoulder nearly touching his.

The sight of that, of her standing with *him,* fired Jax's fury anew.

"June!" he roared. "The game's over! Come to me now!"

She glared at him, and Slade stepped in front of her, his hand resting on the pistol at his hip, his face set hard with grim purpose.

The farm boy was going to play the hero.

"She's not going with you." Slade squared his shoulders.

"This ain't your dance, boy," Jax sneered. "This is between me and what belongs to me."

June flinched. Good. He wanted her to feel it. He wanted her to know what was waiting when she came back.

He nudged his horse forward, his eyes locked on her. "I will not ask again, June."

When she still held her ground, he knew for a fact that this sentimental nonsense had burned away the last bit of the old June. He'd hoped it wouldn't come to this, but she'd forced his hand.

He spurred his horse, meaning to ride straight for her, to snatch her up right in front of her 'protector' and ride off. Before his horse had taken two strides, another shot cracked the air.

It struck his horse.

The animal screamed and went down under him. Jax kicked his boots free of the stirrups, hitting the dusty ground hard. He looked up, stunned for a half-second, his eyes finding the shooter.

Elias.

Smoke curled from his rifle barrel, and he glowered at Jax with a look of savage victory. Jax couldn't tell what satisfaction the man took in shooting his horse instead of him, but it didn't rightly matter. A sheep had found enough teeth to inconvenience him, and he was going to deal with it right now.

Before Jax could bring his own pistol to bear, a shape came at him from the side like a shot from a cannon. Slade smashed into him with bare hands and—in Jax's expert opinion—screams of pure and *dumb* fury. The boy tackled Jax at the waist, and they both went down in a cloud of dust and curses.

Jax grunted, the air knocked out of him.

For a moment, he was seeing stars. Then, he twisted, driving a knee hard into Slade's ribs. The boy gasped, his hold slackening. Jax shoved him off and scrambled to his feet. Cole was up just as quick, his fists raised. He was bigger than Jax had reckoned, lean but wiry strong.

But he was a sheltered town boy.

As Slade came swinging a clumsy but powerful right hook, Jax ducked it easily and drove his own fist into Slade's gut.

Slade folded and wheezed.

"You are *nothing*," Jax hissed.

Grabbing a handful of the boy's hair, Jax slammed his face into the iron rim of a wagon wheel. The boy's nose crunched and gave way, spraying blood as he yelled.

Jax had to give it to him, though—the boy was as stubborn as a mule.

Slade roared and surged back, landing a solid haymaker to Jax's jaw, sending a jolt through his skull. The pain insulted Jax more than it bothered him. It had been a *long* time since any man had laid a hand on him.

No more playing.

Jax pulled the sticker from his boot, the blade flashing in the sun. He lunged, aiming for Slade's gut. But the boy sidestepped, and the knife bit air. Then the boy's fist found Jax's solar plexus, forcing Jax to keel over and exhale. As Jax righted himself, the rest of the train moved in; men with rifles took their positions.

The window to grab June and get out of there had passed.

Shots started ringing out. A bullet buzzed past his ear. Another thudded into the wagon beside him.

"Jax!" Mercy rode up to him. "Get on!"

Jax gave Cole one last look of uncut hatred. This wasn't the end of it. Not by a long shot. He'd lost this little scrap, but the war had just started. He swung up into the saddle behind Mercy.

"Let's go!" he said.

As they wheeled their horses and galloped away, the sounds of shouts and gunfire chasing them, Jax looked back. He saw Cole helping June to her feet, blood streaming from his face. He saw their eyes meet. And, in that moment, his purpose was sharpened down to a fine point.

His mercy had come to an end.

He *would* get her back, and she *would* be his. Before that, however, he'd burn down everything she'd come to care about. He would destroy the wagon train, kill her new friends, and take *special* pleasure in drawing and quartering the boy who thought he could steal her from him.

Chapter Sixteen

July 7th, 1852

Fort Laramie

The world came back to June in fits and starts, like a dream you can't quite shake.

The high-pitched whistle in her ears cleared first, the whine giving way to the hollering of men and the sobbing of women. Then came the stink—acrid gunpowder, hot iron, and the coppery tang of blood that turned her stomach to a knot. The taste of alkali dust caked the back of her throat.

She knelt on the ground, though she had no memory of taking the fall.

Cole stood in front of her, a bright ribbon of blood trickling from his nose, which was already swelling into a bruised lump. His dark eyes fixed on the stretch of trail where Jax and his outfit had vanished into the haze.

Cole had fought for her.

Despite their argument, he stood between her and her personal nightmare and bled to keep her safe. After she'd been nothing but mean to him and only ever insulted his interests and code. How was she supposed to look him in the eyes again?

He leaned down. "You hurt any?"

She shook her head.

A lie. The ache had burrowed into a place no man could see, internal tearing that scraped against her ribcage. She had infected this camp with her problems, and now, all these people she'd come to care about faced danger.

The outfit limped back to Fort Laramie.

The panicked rush of the morning's flight had boiled off, leaving behind a grim quiet. Joe Marlowe walked beside his wagon, constantly sweeping the hills. Pearl and Savannah Calder huddled together, and June noticed the looks they cast her way. Confused glances that asked a question she could never answer.

What kind of devil are you to bring this down on our heads?

Every groan of a wagon wheel and every lowing steer accused June. She stared at the rump of the ox in front of her, focusing on the rhythmic sway of its tail.

Anything to keep from meeting the eyes of the people whose lives she had irrevocably broken.

Cole still infuriated her, however. She appreciated that he'd fought for her, but this was getting ridiculous. His moral code had encountered a challenge, she got that. But it wasn't her fault that Jax was after her.

No one forced Cole to fight for her anyway.

She could take care of herself. Always had, always would. Just 'cause he got his nose broken didn't mean he had the right to judge her or her choices!

Inside the fort's walls, the illusion of safety was paper-thin.

The sounds of a blacksmith's hammer and the distant chatter of soldiers played a performance on a stage—a cheap imitation of a world that no longer existed for her. The train circled up in its designated area like a hurt beast licking its wounds.

Men moved with a heavy-shouldered purpose, easing Boone Travers, still out cold, from a wagon bed.

They carried him to the surgeon's quarters, a low-slung adobe building with a crudely drawn snake on the door. Cole followed despite the exhaustion showing in every line of his body. June followed while glaring at the back of Cole's head.

She had to see this through and see the full measure of the damage she had wrought.

Leaning against the rough wall, she waited outside the surgeon's door and wrapped her arms around herself. Inside, voices murmured, metal instruments clinked, and Travers occasionally groaned. All of it twisted in June's gut.

Travers was a good man. Hard but fair. He'd given her a chance when he had every reason to send her packing, and, for that, Jax had put a bullet in him.

An eternity later, Cole emerged.

He stopped when he saw her, and gawked at her for quite a bit. Anger still churned in his eyes, banking like hot coals, but so did bottomless weariness.

"He'll pull through." Cole shook his head. "Doc dug the lead out. Collarbone's busted. He'll be bedridden for a good long while, but... he'll pull through."

"I'm glad." June nodded. "I would've hated for something to happen to him."

Cole looked at the street. "The sheriff's gonna need a word."

"I know."

"He'll want names. And reasons."

"Cole, I..."

He finally met her eyes, and the look in them silenced her. He resembled a man standing on the edge of a cliff, not sure whether he was going to jump or if someone would push him.

"Come with me," he said.

The ground tilted beneath her. *He's going to turn me in.*

All her life, survival had meant looking out for herself, trusting no one, and running at the first sign of a cage. Now, Cole wanted to take her to the sheriff's office, with its laws and its hangman's ropes. Her instincts screamed at her to bolt, to melt into the fort's evening crowds and disappear into the wild.

But where to? Jax was out there, in the wind. There was no running from him now, not alone.

Cole gently clasped her shoulder. "I want to keep you safe."

She searched his battered face for the lie, and found none. She discovered only stubborn resolve that defied all sense. He still wanted to protect her, even now, after he knew—or she reckoned he knew—the depths of her lies.

Why?

The question handed her a puzzle she couldn't solve, but it was enough. It was a lone candle flame in a black canyon of night.

"Fine." She gave a jerky nod. "Let's go."

***

The sheriff's office smelled of stale cigar smoke, old ink, and the kind of dust that never settled. A pot-bellied stove corroded in one corner, and wanted posters—her own face likely among them somewhere—hung on the wall like tombstones.

The man behind the desk, Sheriff Miller, had the weary face and washed-out eyes of a man who'd seen too much trouble wash up on the shores of his fort. A tin star drooped crookedly to his vest.

For June, the entire room screamed *trap*.

Cole stood before the desk, but June hung back near the door, keeping her escape route clear. The sheriff's eyes passed over her in a dismissive glance that took in her boy's clothes and the grime on her face, and moved on as if she were nothing more than a stray coyote.

Good.

"Sheriff," Cole said. "We were hit. On the trail, not a mile from here. Our wagon master, Boone Travers, took a bullet."

Sheriff Miller rubbed a hand over his face. "Heard the ruckus. Who did the shooting?"

"A gang. They go by the name Thorns."

June held her breath. She watched Cole's back, waiting for him to turn, to point a finger at her.

There she is, Sheriff. That's June Crow. She's one of 'em. The wanted poster proves it.

"Heard tell of 'em. Pack of thieves, mostly." Miller's brow furrowed. "Never heard of 'em being this bold and this close to the fort. What'd they want? Your stock? Supplies?"

"They wanted her." Cole gestured at June without looking at her.

The sheriff's gaze fell on her again, this time with interest. June's skin prickled as if she were an insect pinned to a board.

"What's so special about you, missy?"

131

June's throat dried out. Her life depended on it, but she couldn't speak. She could only stare back with a blank mask that, hopefully, hid her screaming panic.

Cole stepped slightly to the side, putting his body between her and the sheriff's hard stare. "Their leader got a personal score to settle with her. Claimed she was his property. Said he was just collectin'."

He was editing the truth, sanding down the sharp edges, presenting a version of the story that painted her as the prize in some dispute, not a player in the game. Every word he chose protected her from the questions that would lead to the gallows.

Why? Why was he doing this?

Miller grunted, making a note on a piece of paper. "All right. And you fought 'em off?"

"We held our ground. They ran off, but not before he said they'd be back."

Miller shook his head. "And what do you figure *I'm* to do about it, son?"

"We need a posse." Cole put his palms on Miller's desk and leaned forward. "We need to hunt 'em down before they can lick their wounds and come back for another bite."

The sheriff leaned back in his chair. "Son, I'd like to help you, I truly would. But you see this fort? I've got a dozen men to guard it, and half of 'em are as green as spring grass."

"Give us leave to rally some townsfolk then."

"Most of the able-bodied men who ain't soldiers are out at the mines up north, trying to scratch out a living. Ain't no one can go chasing shadows on the prairie right now."

"They're not shadows! They're murderers!" Cole slammed his fist on the desk. "They shot Boone Travers in cold blood! They threatened this entire train! We can't just sit here and wait for them to come back!"

Miller sighed. "Look, there's an army patrol due in from Fort Kearny. Supposed to be here in a day, maybe two. They'll have the men and the horses for a proper pursuit."

"We can't wait!" Cole stepped back. "Our train has a schedule to keep. There are families who need to get over the mountains before the first snow. We're leaving in the morning, with or without your help."

The sheriff's eyes narrowed. "You got sand, kid, I'll give you that. But you're a fool if you think you can take on a gang like The Thorns with a handful of farmers. You'll get yourself and that girl killed."

"That's a risk I'll have to take," Cole said.

He turned and strode out of the office. June, jolted from her stupor, scrambled after him, desperate to escape the suffocating weight of the lawman's gaze.

***

She caught up to him in the alley beside the office. The sun had completely set, and the narrow space was filled with a deep, blue twilight. He stood with his back to her, one hand braced against the adobe wall.

"Cole." She glowered at him. "Turn around and talk to me."

"He meant to kill me. When I was on the ground. I saw it clear in his eyes. He wasn't gonna stop."

"I know."

He turned to face her. "June... who in the hell are they? Not just their names. Who were they... to *you*?"

She took a deep breath.

He wasn't asking as an accuser. He was asking as a man who had bled for a ghost story and now needed to know the truth of it. Her silence had nearly gotten him killed. She owed him this. The wall she had spent a lifetime building, the one made of silence and suspicion and scorn, finally crumbled.

"They were my family." The words filled her mouth with ash. "The only one I ever had. We all grew up together. In an orphanage. A bad place. At first, we were just... strays. No one except each other."

"How'd a band of strays turn into... that?"

"Jax was the oldest. He got us out and taught us how to live. How to... take." She gritted her teeth. "I'd told myself we were surviving. Taking from folks who had plenty to spare. It felt like a game. A dangerous one, but still a game."

"Then Jax... changed?"

"Yes. Something in Jax twisted. Or maybe it was twisted all along, and I was just too young and too dumb to see it." She glanced at her fingers. "He started getting meaner. The robberies got more violent. And then people started dying."

"I understand."

She squeezed her eyes shut, trying to block out the image of the farmer Jax had shot; the man's bewildered face as he crumpled to the ground.

"I thought if I could just get to Oregon, I could start over. Be someone else." She let out a humorless laugh. "Reckon a body can't ever outrun their own shadow."

"You lit out," he said. "As hard as it is for me to deal with it, that makes you different. That's the only thing that matters now."

She looked him straight in the eye. "Nevertheless, they're *my* mistake to own, and I'm going to help you fix it. I'll help you bring them to justice."

Chapter Seventeen

July 8th, 1852

Fort Laramie

Cole had barely slept.

Every time he closed his eyes, he saw Jax Rae's face—the easy, coyote-mean grin twisting into a mask of pure-T killing rage. June, her face a pale moon in the gloom of the inn room, her confession hanging in the air between them like gunpowder smoke.

Outlaw. Thief. Murderer's woman.

She'd told him her story, and he'd come to understand her, but his conscience still wouldn't let it go fully. He was helping a girl who'd stolen, and he'd yet to make his peace with that. Now, as the sun climbed, a new responsibility awaited him.

Boone Travers, the iron spine of their outfit, had broken. The train had lost its head.

"We ought to go see how he's farin'," Joe Marlowe said.

He stood beside Cole within the wagon circle. Behind him, others gathered—the Calder sisters, Elias, and June. June stood a little apart from the rest and stared at some horizon only she could see.

She hadn't looked at him all morning.

Cole nodded at Joe. "Yeah. Let's be about it."

They made their way to the surgeon's quarters in a somber parade.

The gulf between Cole and June had enough width to it for a man to fall in and never hit bottom. He wanted to reach across it, to say something, *anything*, but the words stuck in his throat.

What was there to say? *Sorry I looked at you like you were dirt?*

The surgeon's office was even grimmer in the daylight.

The air was thick enough to chew with the cloying-sweet smell of laudanum and the sharp, clean scent of carbolic acid. Travers lay on a narrow cot, his face the color of old tallow. A thick bandage wrapped around his shoulder and chest, and bound his arm to his side. The poor trail boss stared at the ceiling with the eyes of a whipped man.

"Boone," Joe said softly.

Travers' eyes shifted, focusing on them with a weary effort.

"Joe. Folks." His gaze passed over all of them, lingering for a moment on Cole, then on June, before moving on. "The doc says the lead missed my lights, so I ought to thank my stars. But this bone... it's powder. I won't be liftin' this arm for a long spell. I'm done leadin' this train, and that's the long and short of it."

The news landed with the finality of a spadeful of dirt on a coffin. The hope that had flickered in the camp—that maybe Travers, by some miracle, could still lead them—snuffed out.

Pearl Calder let out a choked sob, which her sister Savannah quickly shushed.

"Then what's the play?" Joe frowned. "We can't let moss grow on us here."

"Pushin' on is a fool's errand." A spasm crossed Travers's face. "Not without a proper head. That trail ahead... she's a widow-maker. The high passes, the river crossings... and with Rae's coyotes sniffin' your tracks... it ain't just suicide. It's a signed invitation to the devil."

"Boone, we all got stakes in the ground out there."

Travers coughed. "The smart money's on bustin' up this outfit. Sell your stock and your rigs. Hole up 'til spring and pray you got enough to try again."

A wave of despair washed through the room. Cole saw it on every face.

To give up now, after everything they had endured? After coming this far? It was unthinkable. They had all staked their entire lives on this journey. For Joe and Lenore, it was a new farm, a future for their daughter. For the Calders, a new homestead and a life away from the ghosts that haunted them back east.

For Cole, it was everything.

For the first time in his life, he'd found a place and earned his keep. To turn back now would be to admit defeat, crawl back to Slade's Way, and tell Luke he'd been wrong about him.

"No." Cole glared at the floor. "It doesn't end like this."

Every head in the room turned to him.

"We ain't quittin'," he said, his voice gaining strength. "We ain't scatterin' to the four winds. We've bled too much for that. We're seein' Oregon country. Every last soul."

Travers exhaled slowly. "And who's gonna point the way, Slade? You? Think you can just aim the pole west and pray? This trail'll chew up a man and spit out his buttons."

"I'll do it." The words tumbled out of Cole's mouth before he'd rightly formed the thought.

They tasted both foreign and completely natural, as if some other man had spoken them through his mouth.

What in God's name did I just say?

Him? A wagon master? He was just a boy who knew how to coax mules and stand up in a scrap. He didn't know the first thing about leading fifty souls through two thousand miles of hell.

"You?" Elias let out a harsh laugh. "You ain't been on this trail long enough to get the dust settled in your lungs. You're a greenhorn, Slade. A pup with a lucky streak, but still wet behind the ears. If any man's got the right, it's me. I've eaten Boone's dust for two full seasons. I know the sweat and the strain of it."

The old tension, the one Cole thought they had buried back at the Shoshone camp, reared its ugly head again. Elias had a point, in a way. He did have more experience. He knew the daily grind of the trail—the practicalities of it—in a way Cole didn't.

But Travers shook his head as he pushed himself up on his good elbow. "No. It's gotta be Slade."

Elias looked as if Travers had slapped him. "What? Boone, that ain't square!"

"The boy's green, I'll grant you. And he's got a fire in his belly that's like to get him shot. But his sand is cool when the bullets are flyin'."

Elias scoffed. "A cool head don't know a safe crossin' from a drownin' hole."

"He puts the herd before himself. He knows the right of a thing and ain't scared to plant his feet for it, no matter how hard the ground." Travers glowered at Elias. "Lead's more than knowin' axle grease from river mud. It's about bein' the bedrock when the whole world's a-tremble. That man is Cole."

Travers' voice brooked no argument. Elias stared at Boone, his face a mask of betrayal and wounded pride, then he turned his glare on Cole. The look simmered with old animosity and a fresh hurt. Without another word, he turned on his heel and stalked out of the room.

A leaden weight settled in Cole's gut. He'd got the job but lost an ally. He had to fix this.

Joe Marlowe stepped forward and put a hand on Cole's shoulder. "Boone's right. We'll follow you, Cole."

Savannah and Pearl murmured their agreement.

Cole gulped. "I won't let you down."

"See that you don't," Travers grunted, sinking back onto the cot. "Now git. All of you. You're burnin' daylight. And Slade... keep your eyes skinned. For Rae... and for the man standin' next to you."

Cole shook his head as he stepped out into the street.

It was kinda ironic. He'd run from the responsibility of taking over Slade's Way, only to find a far heavier one on the trail.

Looks like a man cannot outrun his destiny, even two thousand miles from home.

***

The next morning broke cold and clear.

The air had a sharp, clean bite to it that promised a hard day's travel. Cole had spent the remainder of the previous day in a blur of activity, organizing supplies, checking wagon axles, and speaking with each family.

He'd tried to project a confidence he was a thousand miles from feeling, adopting Travers' firm tone and direct manner. It chafed him like a costume, but he couldn't deny the effect it had. The fear in the camp banked, and determination rose.

He'd tried to talk to Elias, but the man had brushed him off each time.

As Cole dealt with the hitching of the last team of oxen, June emerged from the inn. For a second, he didn't recognize her. She'd discarded the drab dress she'd worn. Instead, she had on a pair of sturdy canvas britches instead, a man's loose-fitting work shirt, and a worn leather vest that looked like it had seen its share of miles.

She looked smaller without the bulk of the skirts, but she also looked right.

The awkwardness she'd always carried in women's clothes had disappeared, and she moved with fluid confidence. It sounded contradictory, but only now, in men's clothes, did June's real inner woman show. It made the damask-and-lace dummy she'd been propping up for show look unnatural.

Cole couldn't take his eyes off her as she walked straight up to him.

"What in tarnation you think you're about?" he said.

She frowned. "Fixin' to ride. What's it look like?"

"No." He shook his head. "You're staying here. It's the safest place for you."

Her eyes narrowed. "Safe? Cole, there ain't a 'safe' spot for me 'twixt here and hell 'til Jax is in the ground. You think these walls will stop him? He'd burn this whole fort down to the dirt for a chance to spit on my ashes."

"I can't be watchin' the trail ahead and my own back trail for you at the same time." He stepped up to her. "I need to know you're out of harm's way."

"And I need to be where I can do some good!" She pushed him back. "I know his mind, Cole. How it twists. I know the men who ride with him. I can smell a deadfall of his a mile off. I ain't baggage, Cole. I'm the card you keep up your sleeve."

"I—"

She closed the distance between them again. "This isn't about you protecting me anymore. We're not engaged, remember? This is about us surviving. Together."

He stared at her, the logic of her words warring with the primal instinct to lock her in a room and stand guard at the door. She was right. He knew she was. To leave her behind would be to leave his best weapon in its sheath. But the thought of her out there, in the line of fire, made his blood run cold.

"I don't like it," he said finally.

"You don't *have* to like it." She smiled. "You just have to trust me."

He let out a long breath. "Fine. But you ride close. You do what I say, when I say it. No arguments."

"Wouldn't dream of it, *trail boss*." She turned and walked toward the supply wagon.

Just as Cole turned back to the oxen, the Calder family made their way to him. Savannah and Pearl glanced at him with knowing eyes. Gideon looked like he'd just swallowed a mouthful of sour milk.

"Mr. Slade." Gideon sniffed. "A word, if I may be so bold. Concerning your... intended."

Cole frowned. "What about her?"

Gideon gestured vaguely in June's direction. "Her attire. It is most unseemly. It is not proper for a woman to present herself in such a masculine fashion."

Cole clenched his jaw. "Mr. Calder, with all due respect, what's proper and what's practical are two different things out here. June's just dressing for the work that needs to be done."

"Hmph," Gideon snorted. "It sets a poor example for decent, God-fearing folk."

With a final, disgusted glance at June, Gideon turned and stalked away.

"Pay him no mind, Cole," Savannah—the older of the two sisters, with a kind and wrinkled face—said, "My brother's heart is in the right place, but his head is stuck back in Missouri."

"That girl's got more grit in her little finger than Gideon has in his whole body," Pearl—who had a mole under her right eye—added with a conspiratorial wink. "I, for one, think she looks ready for a fight. It's a comfort to see."

Cole smiled. "To be honest with you ladies, I'm not sure how to feel about her myself."

Savannah patted his arm. "Love ain't always a church picnic, son. Sometimes it's a storm. A real partnership isn't about how you feel when the sun is shining. It's about who's standing beside you when the lightning cracks the sky."

"You've got yourself a partner in that one, Cole Slade," Pearl said, her eyes twinkling. "Not just some pretty thing to put on a pedestal. She's strong in ways you haven't even seen yet. A man's lucky to have a woman like that at his back. Don't you forget it."

They smiled at him once more and then moved off to their own wagon, leaving Cole standing there with their words ringing in his ears.

A partner.

He'd been so focused on protecting her, on seeing her as a victim to shield or a problem to solve, that he hadn't thought of her as an equal.

He looked over at her again.

She was talking to Joe Marlowe, pointing at a map, her expression focused and intelligent.

He bit his tongue, the whole fool lie of their engagement feeling both heavier and less important than ever before. It didn't matter what the world thought they were. What mattered was what they were forging, right here, in the heart of the fire. And as he gave the final call for the wagons to roll out, leaving the false safety of Fort Laramie behind, he knew one thing with a bone-deep certainty.

Whatever came next, he wouldn't be facing it alone.

Chapter Eighteen

Mid July 1852

West of Fort Laramie

The first morning out of Fort Laramie fed June the coppery taste of fear she knew as well as the worn knife hilt in her palm. Every snap of a whip sounded like a pistol shot. Every call from one driver to another like a warning cry.

She rode the supply wagon, clenching the morning dew-slicked reins so hard her knuckles had gone white. The eyes of the others stabbed into her even when they looked away. Glances that shied away like a spooked horse when she turned her head. Whispers that died when she drew near.

Cole rode on her flank.

Tension lived in his shoulders, his gaze sweeping the rolling hills with an intensity that made her own stomach clench. He had chosen to stand by her, but she had no illusions about the cost. She had fractured the simple, honorable code he carried inside him, and she had no idea if anything could ever piece it back together.

Near midday, when they stopped to water the stock at a muddy creek, Elias braced Cole near the lead wagon. June was checking the lashings on a crate of flour nearby, busying her hands but tuning her ears to them.

"This ain't sittin' right, Slade," Elias bit out. "We're draggin' his marked prey clean across the prairie. We're paintin' a target on our backs for a girl who ain't given a straight accountin' of herself since the day she signed on."

Cole kept a hand on the neck of a thirsty ox. "The matter's settled, Elias. We're bound for the west. The lot of us."

"And what happens when he comes back? When he decides shooting the trail boss ain't enough? You aimin' to hide behind her petticoats then?"

June's hands stilled. Elias had aimed the insult at Cole, but it struck her like a lash. She straightened up, the grit of the flour sack under her fingers a flimsy anchor in a swirling sea of shame and anger. She couldn't let Cole fight this fight for her. Not anymore. Her silence had been a shield, but it had become a cage, and it had nearly gotten him killed.

She walked to them, her boots making soft sounds in the damp earth. Both men turned as she approached. Cole's face was a hard map to read, full of concern and frustration. Elias's was pure, unvarnished suspicion, plain as day.

"Don't put this on him." June glared at Elias. "You knew the whole of it, you'd be glad for my company."

Cole's dark eyes fixed on her. "June, you don't have to—"

"Yes, I do." She stepped between him and Elias. "You figure he's chasin' me on account of some jilted lover's quarrel. That this is wounded pride. It ain't. It's about what I can testify to."

Elias crossed his arms. "And what might that be?"

She took a breath, the air burning her lungs. "I was one of them."

"What?"

"I stole. For years. It was the only way to eat."

Elias focused on Cole. "Slade? Did you know?"

"There was a farmer, back in Missouri." June gritted her teeth. "His wagon was loaded with goods for market. He wouldn't give it up. Jax put a ball in him. Never so much as blinked. Just shot him and had us load our horses."

The color drained from Cole's face. Elias's hostile posture tightened.

"And there was a lawman." June's voice cracked. "A deputy. He got too close to figuring us out. Jax met him on the road. Said they were just going to palaver. He put a bullet in the man's chest and left him for the crows."

Elias glowered at her. "So you're a thief. And you rode with a killer. And you led him right to our campfire."

"I did. Because I could see him do the hangman's jig."

A quiet fell over them, thick as mud, as flies buzzed and the soft sucking sound of the oxen drinking echoed from the creek.

Elias spat on the ground. "I say we stake her out and let him find her. Or hand her over to the law ourselves. She ain't our cross to bear. She's a rattler in the woodpile."

"She's with us." Cole stepped in front of June. "She lit out from him. That's the only count that matters now."

"That's fool talk!" Elias said. "You're soft on her, that's all this is! You're willing to get us all killed for a comely face with a foul history!"

"It's about what's *right*." Cole's jaw tightened. "She's trying to do right, now. That's a chance worth taking."

"A chance that'll get us buried!"

"That's enough."

The voice was calm and steady, and it cut through their argument like a sharp axe through deadwood. Joe Marlowe stood there, having approached them unheard, a bucket of water in his hand. His eyes moved from Elias's angry face, to Cole's determined one, and finally, to June's anxious one.

June flinched under his gaze, expecting to see the same disgust that sprang from Elias's face. She prepared for blame, for this good and decent family man to judge her.

"I've heard the long and the short of it." Joe set the bucket down. "The girl's made her share of wrong turns; the kind I pray my Lily never has to ponder. But I also saw her ride into Fort Kearny for what my wife and child needed, when she could've been savin' her own hide."

June gulped.

Joe smiled at her. "A soul ain't the sum of your blackest day, June. Or even your blackest year. It's about which way you're facin' now. And seems to me, you're facin' the sunrise."

Elias scoffed. "She's ain't worth the danger she—"

"She rides with us. We *protect our own.*" Joe stood next to Cole in front of her. "I stand with Cole."

Elias stared at Joe, his mouth working, but no words came out. June understood. Arguing with Cole, a greenhorn trail boss, was one thing. Contending Joe Marlowe, a man universally respected for his quiet strength and fairness, was another entirely.

With a frustrated grunt, Elias snatched up his rifle and stalked away.

June stood there, her throat tight, and her eyes stinging. For all her problems with Cole, not once had she doubted he would come to her defense. However, she'd never expected *Joe* to come to her aid. See her as a person instead of a problem.

The path ahead was still dark, but for the first time, a small part of her believed she might just find her way through it.

***

The prairie had a mean streak.

As if to mock the fragile truce that had settled over the camp, the land itself decided to fight them. Late in the afternoon, they came to a coulee, a raw gash in the earth a thousand years of rain had carved into the rocks. A recent storm had turned its bottom into a churning bog of hungry mud.

Cole rode to the edge. "No help for it. We gotta ford it."

The first wagon, one of the heavy-supply haulers, went in. The oxen strained, their powerful muscles bunching, their hooves sinking deep. The wagon lurched, groaned, and then, with a sound like a dying beast, settled. Its wheels sank into the brown muck up to the axles.

A collective groan went up from the train.

Men shouted advice, oxen bellowed, and June's mind pitched her to the start of the journey.

'No skin off *my* nose', she had said as she watched Cole run to help that other family with their tipped wagon. How foolish she had found him, mixing in that fool's errand. *She'd* been the fool.

Cole had been right all along.

Without a second thought, she slid down from her wagon seat, her boots landing in the soft earth at the edge of the coulee. Ignoring the surprised look from Savannah Calder, who was wringing her hands nearby, June waded into the mud.

It sucked at her boots, trying to pull her down. She pushed through it, her eyes on the chaos. Cole was there, up to his shins in the muck, trying to calm the lead steer. Joe and a few other men were putting their shoulders to the wheel, a futile gesture against so much dead weight.

"It ain't gon' budge like that!" June walked up to them. "You'll break the yoke!"

Cole looked over, his face smeared with dirt. "Got a better idea, do you?"

"The purchase is all wrong!" She pointed at it. "We need to pull it sideways first, get the front wheels on that bit of hardpan there. We need more rope, and we need to hitch another team to the side, not the front."

It was the kind of practical, spatial logic she'd learned from years of watching Jax and the others figure out how to move heavy goods in the dead of night. It was a scoundrel's knowledge, but right now, it was useful.

Cole hesitated for only a second, then nodded. "Do it!"

Giving orders tasted strange, but the men listened. Maybe it was the iron in her voice, or maybe they were just desperate enough to try anything.

She directed them, pointing out the best place to anchor a rope to the wagon's frame, showing them how to double-loop it for strength. Working alongside them, she grabbed the coarse rope and pulled, the strain jarring her shoulders.

Elias, it seemed, had forgotten his anger in the face of the immediate trouble. He stood on the other side of the wagon, and their eyes met over the canvas top. He gave a curt, almost imperceptible nod. She was sure he hadn't forgiven her, but he *had* acknowledged her.

For now, that was enough.

They all heaved, their grunts harmonizing with the straining of the steer. The mud fought them like a living thing that refused to release its prize.

"Now! Together!" Cole roared.

June dug her heels in, her muscles screaming. With a great gasp, the wagon shifted. It moved only a foot, but it sent a ragged cheer up in the group. With the new angle, the combined pull of the two teams of steer, and the shoulders of every able-bodied man, the wagon groaned, protested, and finally crawled its way out of the coulee's grip and onto the solid ground of the far side.

June panted, covered in mud from head to toe, and looked around at the small army who'd just won a war against a ditch. She giggled as Joe clapped Cole on the back, and they both laughed. Someone offered June a canteen, and she drank deeply, water washing the grit from her teeth.

***

Later that evening, as she sat by the fire, tending to her aching bones and the raw hide of her palm, she exhaled slowly. Jax still loomed out there, sure, but the pit in her gut had lessened.

She looked at her hands, calloused and dirty from a day of honest work.

She had helped. She had put her shoulder to the wheel, literally, for the sake of the group, and it hadn't made her weak. Well, she didn't think it made her weak. She didn't *feel* weak.

It had made her... one of them.

Across the fire, Cole talked to Lily Marlowe, his battered face breaking into a genuine smile as the little girl showed him a rock she'd found. When he looked up and caught June watching, he smiled.

That one smile had more value to it than any stolen coin.

Chapter Nineteen

Mid July 1852

Deeper West of Fort Laramie

The mud from the coulee had dried and caked to Cole's britches and the creases of his knuckles. He'd washed his face and hands, of course, but the grit of it had dug a trench and refused to leave it.

He felt good, though.

The ache in his shoulders from hauling on the ropes, the scrape on his palm where the rope had bit him—they were the wages of a hard day's work done together. For the first time since leaving Fort Laramie, the outfit didn't simmer like a pot about to boil over.

Cole nursed a tin of coffee, one that had more chicory than bean, by the fire and watched the camp come to life. Joe Marlowe checking the yoke on his oxen. Pearl and Savannah laughing about something. Elias grumbling about his chores.

He looked for June.

She was seeing to the harness on one of the lead mules, wearing her new buckskins as if she'd been born in them. This kind of confidence really suited her.

She must have felt his gaze, because she looked up.

Their eyes met across the bustling camp. There had been a wall of anger and betrayal that had stood between them since the inn had crumbled, but a skittish quiet had taken its place. Cole couldn't put his finger on why. They had no more secrets from each other, yet they skittered around each other like frightened rabbits.

If he didn't know better, he'd start thinking—

"Riders!" Elias, perched on the seat of a high wagon, called out.

The brittle peace of the morning cracked wide open. Instantly, the camp turned into a cyclone of movement. Joe fetched the rifle that always leaned against his wagon wheel. The Calder sisters scooped up kids from their play, herding them behind the relative safety of the wagons. Men dropped what they were doing, their hands going to the sidearms at their belts.

Cole dropped his tin and laid hands on the Henry rifle, litting out for the front of the wagon circle, his mind racing.

This couldn't be Jax. He'd be too cunning for a frontal approach like this.

Squinting against the morning sun, Cole took a gander out past the lead wagon. A dozen riders approached at a steady pace, kicking up a tail of dust that hazed their shapes.

"Hold your fire!" Cole raised his arm. "Wait on my word!"

June walked up to him with a shooting iron of her own in her hand.

As the riders drew closer, the details began to resolve. Rangy ponies, not the Thorns' heavy-boned horses. The men rode bareback, with a fluid grace that spoke of a lifetime riding. Their skin was the color of the sun-scoured earth, their black hair long and unbound. The Shoshone.

Cole frowned.

The lead rider held up a hand, and the group halted a respectful fifty yards from the wagons. He was an older man, his face a roadmap of hard years, his eyes deep-set and intelligent. A fresh, mean-looking gash ran down his forearm, the blood dried to a dark crust.

Cole stepped up with his barrel pointing at the ground in a sign of peace. "That's far enough. State your business."

The lead rider dismounted and walked forward alone. "You are the leader of this train?"

"I am," Cole said. "Cole Slade."

"I am Keme. My folk camped by the river, two nights past. We saw your fires."

"We meant no trouble."

"Trouble found us all the same." Keme gestured back toward his men, several of whom bore wounds. "Four men. They came in the dark. They thought we were fat with trade goods from the fort. They tried to take our horses."

A chill took Cole. "The Thorns."

Keme's eyes narrowed. "You know these men?"

June stepped up beside him. "We know 'em. They're a bad bunch, poison to the core."

"You have brought a nest of snakes into this land." Keme looked at Cole and the entire train of prairie schooners with a look of deep contempt. "Your people come here, with your iron plows and your wagons that scar the earth. You say you seek a new life, but you bring your old sickness with you. Your greed. Your lawlessness. You cannot even control your own kind."

The words bit Cole like a whip crack. He felt a hot tide of protest rising in his throat. He wanted to argue, to say they weren't like Jax, that they were good people, God-fearing families. He wanted to tell this man about Luke Slade and the lessons of honor and decency he'd been raised on.

But the words died before they were born.

Because what defense was there? Jax *was* their kind. The trouble *had* followed them. They *had* brought the sickness here, whether they'd meant to or not. Keme's accusation was a hard, simple truth, and it struck at the very heart of Cole's belief in the rightness of their journey.

"We ain't them." Cole gulped. "We aim to put 'em in the ground."

Keme let out a short, harsh sound that might have been a laugh. "You will stop the wind from blowing? You travel in your slow wagons like turtles waiting for the hawk."

CRACK!

The sound was sharp, flat, and final. It came from the high ground to their left, from a rocky outcrop a few hundred yards away. The man behind Keme jerked violently with a look of stunned surprise on his face, toppling from his pony like a sack of grain. A dark stain blossomed from his deerskin shirt.

Chaos broke loose.

Shoshone ponies screamed and reared. Women in the wagon train shrieked. Gunfire erupted from the rocks, bullets spitting up dust around them, whining through the air with the sound of angry hornets.

"Cover!" Cole heaved Keme to the safety of the wagons.

Before, his first instinct would've been to take June, but he'd seen her competence. Already, she had run off to direct families to hide behind the thick wagon wheels. Dropping to one knee beside Joe, Cole scanned the ridge for attackers and found them crouching behind a group of rocks.

This was more up Jax's alley.

Joe was already returning fire, his face set like hardpan. Elias was on the other side, shucking shells into his rifle with a speed born of pure adrenaline. The outfit had more guns, but the Thorns had the better position.

"They got the high ground!" Elias shouted over the din. "They'll whittle us down one by one!"

Cole glanced at the Shoshone. Keme was shouting orders in his own tongue, his men rallying with a discipline that shamed the outfit's own panicked scramble. They were warriors, and they were now in a fight for their lives because of Cole and *his* train.

Jax stood up from behind a rock.

From this distance, Cole couldn't see his face, but he could imagine the smug grin on that son of a gun's face. A man like that would be enjoying all the terror and bloodshed.

Another bullet thudded into the wagon beside Cole, sending splinters flying. Jax broke away from the others, moving along the ridge and disappearing behind a swell of land. He was flanking them, or maybe... maybe he was just running.

No, not running. He was leading Cole on. It was a private invitation.

My charge is to the train, a voice that sounded like Luke Slade whispered in his head. *Protect the flock.*

But June's face flashed in his mind. Jax was the wolf. If Cole killed him now, June would be safe.

"Elias! Joe! Keep 'em busy!" Cole yelled.

He sprinted for his horse, tethered just inside the wagon circle. He swung into the saddle, the Henry rifle feeling like an extension of his arm. Shoshone broke off, several warriors on their fast ponies streaking toward the ridge to engage The Thorns on their own terms.

That bought him his chance.

He spurred his horse, leaning low over its neck, and galloped out of the circle, angling toward the spot where he'd last seen Jax. The wind whipped at his face, the sound of the gunfire fading behind him, replaced by the pounding of his horse's hooves and the frantic beating of his own heart.

This was foolish. Reckless. A trail boss didn't abandon his charge to run down a personal devil.

But Cole was more than a trail boss. He was the man who had looked into the face of pure evil and had promised, to himself and to the terrified girl that needed his help, that he would see it brought to justice.

He rounded the swell of land, the prairie opening up before him. And there was Jax, a hundred yards ahead, his horse at a full gallop. He glanced back over his shoulder, and even from this distance, Cole could see the mocking laughter on his face.

Jax was playing with him.

Cole dug his heels in, urging his horse faster, the ground blurring beneath him. The world narrowed to the space between him and the man he now knew he was put on this earth to stop. The dust, the wind, the straining muscles of his horse, the cold weight of the rifle in his hands—it was all that existed.

He was no longer a boy running from responsibility. He was a man riding toward it, at a dead run, with a prayer on his lips and murder in his heart.

The gap between them closed agonizingly slowly. Fifty yards. Forty. Cole raised the rifle, trying to draw a bead on the bouncing figure, a near-impossible shot.

Jax chose that moment to veer sharply, guiding his horse into a narrow, stony draw that snaked into the hills. Cole followed without hesitation, his horse skidding on the loose rock as they entered the tight confines of the canyon.

The chase was desperate, a mad dash through a world of stone and shadow. Jax was a better rider, his movements fluid and confident, while Cole felt clumsy, his horse fighting for footing. Jax was always just ahead, a fleeting shadow, his laughter bouncing off the canyon walls, a sound that would curdle a man's blood.

Cole was losing him.

With a final, defiant yell, Jax spurred his horse up a steep, treacherous game trail that climbed the canyon wall. Cole's horse, its lungs heaving, its sides lathered white with sweat, couldn't follow. It stumbled, nearly going to its knees.

Cole pulled back on the reins, his own breath coming in ragged, burning gasps. He sat there, helpless, and watched as Jax reached the top of the ridge. Jax paused for a moment, a stark silhouette against the pale sky. He raised a hand, not in a wave, but in a final, mocking salute. Then he was gone.

Cole slammed his fist against his thigh, a raw sound of frustration tearing from his throat.

He had failed. He'd had him, and he'd let him get away.

Slowly, his shoulders slumping with the weight of his exhaustion and defeat, he reined his horse about and began the long, slow ride back to the wagon train. He didn't know what he would find.

He only knew that this would happen again.

Chapter Twenty

Late July 1852

West of Fort Laramie

Jax lay on his belly atop a low rise, the grit of the earth pressing into the rough wool of his duster. The bitterness of incompetence scorched the back of his tongue. He despised that flavor more than any other.

His tools had failed him.

He ran an oiled rag down the barrel of his Colt, the methodical motion a small island of order in a sea of his own simmering rage. The scent of gun oil was clean. Honest. It was the smell of purpose. Down below, hidden in a scrub-choked arroyo, the rest of his "family" were licking their wounds like whipped curs. Clay was sullen, Griffin was sanctimonious, and Mercy was sharp-edged and silent, which was somehow the most irritating of all.

They'd let a handful of dirt-scratching farmers and a pack of half-naked savages on ponies best them.

The memory of it, of pulling back from the fight with nothing to show for it but empty cartridges and the Shoshone's echoing war cries, was a hot coal in his gut. He had miscalculated. He had underestimated the fight in them, and he had overestimated the spine in his own crew.

A crunch of boots on the gravelly soil announced their approach.

He didn't have to look up. He could *feel* Griffin's righteous indignation radiating off him like heat from a forge. Clay would be a step behind, a loyal and stupid shadow. Mercy would be hovering, watching, her silence a judgment all its own.

Griffin stood above him. "Jax, this has to stop."

Jax finished wiping down the cylinder of his revolver, clicking it back into place with a satisfying snap. He still didn't look up. Let him stew. Let him choke on his own pointless morality.

"We're miles from anywhere," Griffin said. "Every lawdog and bounty man west of the Missouri's got our name now. All on account of a gal who plainly wants us gone."

"Mind your jaw, Griffin." Clay sniffed. "You're talking about June."

"I'm talkin' about our own hides!" Griffin sighed. "She picked her trail. Let her ride it!"

Mercy crossed her arms. "Griffin."

"Let us go back to what we're good at." Griffin swallowed. "There's payrolls in Missouri just waitin' for a visit. A man could live fat. Instead, we're out here chewin' grit and dodgin' hot lead on account of your pride gettin' nicked!"

Jax slowly rose to his feet, turning to face them.

He brushed the dirt from his duster. He looked at Griffin, at the sweat on his brow, at the way his hand trembled slightly where it rested near his pistol.

"Pride?" Jax circled him. "You been ridin' with me all these years, Griffin, and your thoughts are still that damn small?"

"I know what you're going to say, but—"

"There ain't no 'buts'!" Jax stopped in front of Griffin, invading his space. "I will not risk it!"

"She wouldn't talk," Griffin mumbled, his gaze falling to his boots. "She's one of us."

"She *was*," Jax's voice turned to ice. "Now she's a stray dog. And a stray gets hungry. Gets scared. A scared, hungry dog'll turn on its own damn master for a scrap of meat and a warm fire."

Griffin frowned. "Then we should have put her in the ground already. You had the shot. This *chase* is what's going to get us caught. It's personal for you, Jax. Admit it."

That was it. The final line. The accusation that this was about feeling, about sentiment. The ultimate insult.

Jax backhanded Griffin across the face, the crack of his knuckles against bone sharp and loud in the quiet air. Griffin stumbled back, a look of pure shock on his face, a trickle of blood starting from his lip.

Before he could recover, Jax followed, grabbing a fistful of Griffin's shirt and slamming him back against a rock outcropping. Griffin's head hit the stone with a dull thud. Jax pressed the muzzle of his Colt hard under Griffin's chin, forcing his head up.

"This crew," Jax hissed, his face inches from Griffin's, "is a machine *I* built. Out of mud and spit and pieces no one else had a use for. You. Clay. Mercy. And her. I built it. And when a gear in the works goes bad, threatens to grind the whole thing to a halt, you don't just toss it aside. You don't get soft. You beat it back into shape. You understand me?"

Griffin's eyes widened as he nodded.

"Good." Jax released him, holstering his pistol.

Griffin slid down the rock face, coughing and wiping the blood from his mouth with the back of his hand.

Jax turned to the others. Clay looked on with grim approval. He understood the simple logic of dominance. Mercy watched with her usual unreadable expression, but Jax saw a flicker of satisfaction in her eyes. He looked out across the prairie, his mind already working, discarding the failed plan and building a new one, a better one, from its ashes.

"They'll be heading west, toward the South Pass. The trail gets tight in the foothills. Ravines. Canyons. Places where a train of clumsy wagons is nothing but a coffin on wheels." A cold smile spread across his face. "Clay. That dynamite we lifted from the mining supply store in Independence. How much do we have left?"

Clay's face lit up. "Three sticks, Jax. And plenty of fuse."

"Perfect," Jax said. "Find me a spot. A ravine with no way out."

***

The place Clay found was a masterpiece of natural cruelty.

A long, winding ravine, its walls sheer and crumbling, just wide enough for a wagon to pass. It was a trap God himself must've prepared for Jax, and Jax was going to spring it. They spent the better part of the day getting into position, working with a renewed sense of purpose. Even Griffin went about his task without complaint, his face bruised and swollen.

They set the charges on a high ledge overlooking a narrow bend in the trail, a spot where the lead wagons would be committed, with no room to turn back. Clay, with his simple, brutal efficiency, handled the dynamite, while Jax chose their vantage point, a nest of rocks that gave them a perfect, unobstructed view.

Then they waited.

That was the hardest part. The sun beat down, baking the rocks until they were hot to the touch. The wind whispered through the ravine, carrying the scent of dust and dry grass. Jax lay on his stomach, the spyglass pressed to his eye, and felt the familiar, cold patience settle over him.

He was a craftsman, about to apply his art.

This wasn't just about violence. It was about psychology. Breaking their will, shattering their pathetic little community, and showing June the folly of her choice.

He thought of Cole Slade.

The orphan boy playing at being a man. The boy who had stood in front of June, who had tackled him, who had dared to bleed on him. The contempt Jax felt was a physical thing, a sour taste in his mouth.

Slade represented everything Jax had clawed his way up from. That naive belief in right and wrong, that misplaced faith in others. He was a walking, talking embodiment of the weakness that got men killed in this world. And he had infected June with his sickness.

Late in the afternoon, he saw them.

A slow-moving snake of canvas and wood, crawling into the mouth of the ravine. His heart began to beat a little faster, a drummer calling his blood to battle. He adjusted the spyglass, bringing them into sharp focus.

There was Slade, riding near the front, and beside him... Jax's knuckles went white where he gripped the spyglass. Riding beside him, on her own horse, was June. She was out front. Right in the kill zone.

A hot, vicious conflict roared to life inside him. Part of him, the cold, pragmatic part, knew it didn't matter. She was part of the lesson now. She had chosen them. If she was caught in the blast, then that was the price of her disloyalty. She had to learn.

But another part, a deeper, more possessive part, recoiled. She was *his*. His creation. His most valuable possession. To see her there, so vulnerable, so close to the fire... it was like watching someone take a hammer to a priceless diamond.

"She's too close," Griffin whispered from beside him.

"She chose her spot," Jax said, his own voice sounding distant, as if it belonged to someone else.

He watched her, the way she sat her horse, the determined set of her jaw. She was looking forward, toward a future he wasn't a part of. And that was the thing that sealed it.

He lowered the spyglass.

The internal debate was over. If he couldn't have her whole, he would have her broken. He would scour Slade's influence from her with fire and terror, and if she didn't survive the lesson, then at least the boy wouldn't have her either.

"Wait for the third wagon to pass the bend," he said. "Clay. When I give the signal. Not a second before."

The wagons crawled forward, their progress agonizingly slow. The seconds stretched into an eternity. The lead wagon. The second. The third, a heavy conestoga with patched canvas that belonged to the two widowed sisters, lumbered past the bend.

"Now," Jax said.

He raised the spyglass to his eye just as Clay touched the burning end of a cheroot to the fuse. He watched the spark fizzle, race down the line.

The world erupted.

The blast was more a concussion than a sound, a physical blow that he felt in his teeth and bones. The ledge where they had set the charges disintegrated, sending a tidal wave of rock and dirt cascading down into the ravine. It slammed into the widows' wagon with the force of God's own fist.

The wagon vaporized, exploding into a cloud of splinters, canvas, and the contents of a life scattered to the four winds. The horses screamed, a terrible, high-pitched sound that was cut short. The shockwave hit the other wagons, knocking them sideways, throwing people from their seats.

Through the settling dust, Jax saw it all. People scrambling, screaming. The train was broken, crippled. The front half was cut off from the back. It was a masterpiece.

His eyes found June. Her horse had thrown her, and she was on the ground, struggling to rise. And then he saw Slade. The boy was running straight for June. Jax watched, his breath catching in his throat, as Slade reached her, knelt beside her, helped her to her feet. Jax glared as the boy put a hand on her arm. As June leaned on him.

Something in Jax snapped.

"Let's go." He scrambled to his feet and pulled his pistol. "We ride. We finish them. Now!"

"Jax, wait!" Mercy grabbed his arm. "Riders!"

He looked where she was pointing. Cresting a hill a half-mile away, coming hard, was a line of horsemen. Blue uniforms. A glint of sun on a brass bugle. The sheriff's posse. That meddling fool from Laramie had actually done it.

The rage curdled into a cold, black frustration. The timing was impossible. A few more minutes. That's all he'd needed. A few more minutes to ride down there and put a bullet in the boy's head right in front of her.

"Damn it all to hell," Griffin breathed, already backing away.

Jax stared down at the scene, at the smoke and the chaos, at Cole and June standing together, a small island of defiance in the wreckage he had wrought.

He had lost the moment.

He scowled, the taste of ash in his mouth. He looked at his crew, at their pale, frightened faces. They were right. To attack now, with a posse bearing down on them, was suicide.

With a final, lingering look of pure, uncut hatred at the two figures below, Jax turned away.

"We'll wait," he said, his voice a low growl that promised future bloodshed. "Let them think they're safe. Let them bury their dead. This isn't over."

Chapter Twenty-One

Late July 1852

The camp after the dynamite explosion

June awoke in fits and starts, like looking at her reflection in the shards of broken glass. The first thing she knew for certain was the ringing in her ears, a whistle like wind through a crack in a cabin wall.

Then taste.

A paste of alkali dust caked her tongue and the back of her throat. She tried to swallow, but the muscles seized up and refused to obey.

Dizziness washed over her, and she realized she lay on the ground. Hard-packed earth cooled her shoulder and poked her skin.

The memory of the blast came next, though it rang through her head as a feeling instead of a proper memory. The world-shaking roar, the shove of air that had plucked her from her horse's back and thrown her like a cornhusk doll.

"June! June, talk to me!"

The voice cut through the whistle. Close. Urgent. A comfort she hadn't earned.

She pried her eyes open.

Cole knelt over her. A deep gash was open on his cheekbone, and his nose had swollen to purplish ruin, but his dark eyes fixed on her. His hands hovered over her as if she were a piece of fine porcelain he was scared to breathe on, let alone touch.

"You busted up?" He looked concerned. "Anything broken?"

She shook her head, the jolt sending fresh pain through her skull. "No. I... I reckon not."

With a grunt that scraped her raw throat, she pushed herself into a sitting position. Her vision tilted something fierce for a moment before it settled.

That's when she took in the full scope of the devastation.

The ravine had become an image straight from hell. Dust and smoke hung in the air, burning her nostrils with the chemical tang of dynamite. Men shouted, their voices tightening with panic that had teeth. Further down the wagon line, a woman was screaming.

The widows' wagon, however, stole breath from her lungs.

It lay on its side like a wounded steer with its back broken. It lacked a wheel, two others had cracked, and the canvas had burned into a blackened and shredded mess. A dark stain pooled near the wreckage.

"Dear Lord," June whispered, the words catching in her neck. "Pearl... Savannah..."

Cole's jaw clenched, his gaze following hers. "Joe and some of the others are with them. The sheriff's men, too."

She gawped at the frantic cluster of figures around the overturned wagon.

Joe knelt, burying his face in his hands as if he could block out the sight. Gideon Calder stood nearby, his face ashen and his body as stiff and brittle as old firewood.

June stared as two of the sheriff's men carefully lifted a limp form from the wreckage.

Pearl.

Even from this distance, June could see that her arm was bent at an angle that God had never intended. Savannah was right behind them, her face a mask of horror.

This is my fault.

Every scream, splinter of wood, and drop of blood soaking into Nebraska soil added another tally to her ledger. She had brought this plague down upon these people. These good, decent people who had offered her a place and looked at her with kindness she'd never known before.

Cole helped her to her feet. "Come on. Let's get you clear of the worst of it."

As he pulled her towards a cluster of boulders where some of the knot of men jawing near the center of the chaos snatched her attention, Sheriff Miller stood toe-to-toe with Elias, their voices rising over the general din.

"—a fool's errand, Miller! Riding us straight into a hornet's nest!" Elias gestured wildly at the smoldering wagon. "Your lawmen were meant to be our guard, not our undertakers!"

"We didn't know they was packin' dynamite, son, how could we?" The sheriff gritted his teeth. "This ain't some back-alley tussle. They were lyin' in wait."

"And I'm wonderin' who they were layin' for!" Gideon said.

He left his sisters' side and stalked over to the argument, pointing a trembling finger at June. "The trouble's been dogging our steps since the day *she* signed on! We've been cursed by her presence! She's brought the devil himself to our camp!"

Heads turned. Eyes found her. The Marlowes, the other families, their faces a mix of fear, confusion, and dawning suspicion. They looked at her as the source of their misery. The snake in their midst.

Cole's grip on her arm tightened. "Don't you listen to him, June. He's just scared and lookin' for someone to blame."

But she knew Gideon had a point. Her past was a sickness, and everyone who got close enough caught the fever.

She pulled her arm from Cole's grasp. "He ain't wrong."

Turning away from him, she left the heart of the camp, her legs moving on their own.

***

She found a flat rock near the edge of the ravine, far enough away to be alone but close enough to still witness the wreckage she'd caused.

Sinking onto it, she wrapped her arms around her stomach as if to physically hold her splintering self together.

She watched as the surgeon who traveled with the sheriff's party tended to Pearl. Lenore Marlowe clutched Lily to her chest and whispered reassurances into the little girl's hair while her own eyes were afraid. Joe and Elias try to right the broken wagon, their faces glaring at the futility of it all.

Cole had sworn to protect these people.

He'd built a community around them with sheer stubbornness and relentless decency. June kept pulling it apart at the seams.

Her old instincts screamed at her.

Run. Skedaddle. Melt into the wilderness and save your own hide.

The lesson the orphanage had worked so hard to teach her and the creed the Thorns had hammered into her head.

Look out for your own self, because no one else will.

Now that she thought about it, Jax really should've come up with a better creed if he'd wanted her.

Not that she would do it either.

Running now would be the most profound sort of cowardice. It would mean leaving this disaster for Cole to clean up. Abandoning these people to a fate she had delivered to their doorstep. The thought of it churned in her gut like boiling poison.

She had only one choice.

Leave, yes, but without hiding. She had to ride out of here loudly enough for the Thorns to notice and follow her. Lead them on a chase deep into the wild country until either they caught her or she managed to disappear for good.

As far as plans went... it could be better.

All of them rode *and* knew the land as well as she did. The chances of her escaping were about as good as Cole declaring his love and asking her to marry him right now.

Yet, she had to do it.

Doomed to fail or not, she would find her courage for these people. The peace of her own soul and sleep with no regrets, giving her nightmares. For *Cole.*

As the decision settled in her bones, her limbs stopped trembling.

***

A pair of worn boots appeared in her line of sight. She looked up. Cole stood in front of her, shadows falling over his face in the fading light. He held a canteen in one hand and a strip of clean cloth in the other.

"Here." He offered her a rag wet with whisky. "You're bleeding."

She blinked. She hadn't even noticed.

He knelt in front of her and dabbed at the cut with the damp cloth. His large hands moved with care, and he murmured words she couldn't make out but assumed came from his days in his orphanage.

I wonder whether it was something someone said to him or he said to others.

Watching him work, she took a deep breath. "I'm leaving, Cole."

He paused, the cloth hovering an inch from her skin. "What's that you say?"

"Tonight. I'm takin' a horse and makin' tracks." She glanced at him. "I'll draw him off. Away from all of you."

His dark eyes searched her face. "No. You ain't."

"You can't stop me," she said. "Ain't no other way."

"Like hell there ain't."

"Long as I'm with this train, no one's safe. Just look around you, Cole! Look what my shadow's brought down on you today!"

"We'll handle it."

174

"Pearl's arm's all busted!" She jumped up. "That blast could've taken Joe, or that little girl. It could've taken *you*!"

"June, please." He stood up with his hands raised. "We can figure—"

"This is *my* cross to bear. My ghost to put in the ground. I won't have any more blood in my ledger."

"So, what's the plan? Ride out there and let him put you in the ground?" He glared at her. "Play the saint for us?"

"The plan is to buy you all time. Time to get to Oregon and build what you set out to do," she said. " Jax wants me. He'll follow. That's the only sure thing in this godforsaken world."

"I ain't lettin' you go." He walked up to her and grabbed her shoulders. "We started this ride together, and we'll see the end of it together."

"There ain't no 'we' in this!" She pushed him away. "Don't you see it? *I'm* the Jonah! I'm why Travers got shot, why Pearl's arm is broke to hell, why every decent soul here is watchin' the horizon for the next fight!"

"I don't care."

"Watchin' after me is a fool's game, Cole. I've let you play it long enough."

He held the side of her head. "Then I'll play the fool."

"You've got a duty to these folks!" She gestured to the camp. "You're the trail boss! You can't just up and chase after me!"

"They'll be safe enough with the sheriff's men and Elias. You ain't out there. Not with Jax on your trail."

"I can handle myself without you."

"I know." His thumb rubbed the side of her head. "But I'd never draw another easy breath knowin' I let you ride into that alone."

Tears pricked at her eyes, and she glowered at him even as her belly filled with warmth. "I can't ask you to risk your own neck for my mess."

"You ain't asking." His gaze was intense, unwavering. "I'm tellin' you. I'm with you, come hell or high water."

He took a half step back, giving her room to breathe, but his eyes held her fast.

"You're right on one count." He observed the distance. "You know how he thinks. You know his ways. I've learned a bit about fighting on his trail. We can kill him. Together."

She watched him.

Only now did she realize she'd never *seen* him before. A naive orphan and a do-gooder who couldn't help but rush into trouble, yes. Now, she noticed the man.

One with a battered face and a spine of steel, who was willing to walk into the fire *with* her, not just *for* her. He *knew* her. Someone who would've offered to save her.

Cole was proposing to stand by her.

The fight drained out of her. For the first time in her life, she had someone with her who wanted to help her *and* push her to be a better person. The realization both terrified and freed her.

She let out a shaky breath. "Alright, Cole."

He smiled and pressed his forehead to hers.

"Alright." She smiled. "We go together."

Chapter Twenty-Two

Late July 1852

In the wilderness, heading toward the Sweetwater River valley

June and Cole's decision spread through the camp like a thief, passing from wagon to wagon in hushed tones and somber glances, sneaking on the cold morning air like a funeral dirge.

Cole still didn't find this the best idea. Cutting themselves from the herd would draw the wolves away, but it would also leave Cole and June vulnerable.

Not much to do about it now.

He'd accepted her decision and promised to follow her, so he'd do that. He'd fight and bleed at her side. Win or lose, live or die, whatever happened, they'd both suffer the same fate.

He packed a light. Two bedrolls, a sack of coffee, hardtack and jerky, a skillet, and as much ammunition as two horses could carry. Yet, even as he moved through the motions of preparing, his mind galloped a thousand miles away.

Every task stung like a betrayal.

He'd told June the wagon train would be safe with the sheriff and Elias, and it *would*, but Cole had promised to be their trail boss. He'd stood in front of Travers and asked for this responsibility.

Now, he'd chosen June over them.

The goodbyes hurt the most. They came to him one by one, telling him they understood even as their eyes watered and their voices trembled.

Joe wrung his hand with a hard grip. "Ride straight and shoot true, Cole. You got more sand than I do."

Next to them, Lenore pulled June into a fierce hug that made her stiffen before she awkwardly patted the woman's back.

"You keep him out of his own fool head, you hear?" Lenore whispered. "That boy's got a stubborn streak wider than the Platte River."

I'm pretty sure I wasn't supposed to hear that.

Lily trotted up and pressed a smooth river stone into Cole's hand. "For good luck."

Cole's throat closed up. He curled his fingers around the stone, its weight echoing the familiarity of the one he carried from Luke.

Another connection, another departure.

The Calder sisters approached next. Pearl's arm sat in a sling, and her face remained pale, but she offered a wobbly smile.

Savannah patted his arm. "Mind how you go, Cole Slade. Told you a storm was brewin'. Best you two ride it out together."

Gideon sniffed a few feet away. He'd turned his back to them, pretending to check the cinch on his saddle, but he glanced over occasionally.

Cole knew what Gideon thought of June, despite her choosing to leave. He saw a Jezebel, a bringer of ruin, and Cole almost punched him for it, but stopped himself for Pearl and Savannah's sake, because he and June were leaving.

Had June chosen to stay, Gideon would be sporting a black eye right about now.

Elias approached last. He stopped a few feet away, wearing a complicated mix of resentment and grudging respect on his face.

"Slade."

"Blackthorn."

"You watch your back trail." Elias peeped at the empty plains in the distance. "That Rae fellow... he ain't the kind to fight square."

"I'll keep a weather eye," Cole looked past Elias, to the long line of wagons and the faces of the families staring back at him. "You get these folks to Oregon. That's your charge now."

Elias nodded.

They would never get closer to a truce than that. Heck, they'd likely never see each other again even if Cole and June did kill the Thorns. Yet, Cole felt as if they'd finally grown to understand each other.

Two young men bearing burdens and responsibilities they hadn't asked for.

***

The time came.

Nothing left to do but turn their backs and ride.

Cole swung into his saddle with a creak of leather and glimpsed at June. She had already mounted and was watching the western horizon, her face set in stone.

She looked as if she were riding to her own execution.

Cole nudged his horse forward, and she fell in beside him. They rode out of the canyon's meager shadow and into the unforgiving emptiness of the prairie, the sounds of the wagon train fading behind them until nothing remained apart from the clip-clop of two horses and the sigh of the wind through the tall grass.

The quiet got under Cole's skin first.

For weeks, his world had played a symphony of noise. The groan of wagon wheels, the lowing of oxen, the chatter of families, the crackle of a communal fire. It had sounded like life.

Now, he had only June and two horses to listen to under a sky so vast it made him feel like a single speck of dust in God's great wilderness.

He'd wanted adventure.

To be on his own. He'd told himself he was a loner at heart, but he now knew that to be a boy's foolish fancy.

He'd spent his entire life surrounded by the noise and bustle of thirty other boys at Slade's Way. He was no more a loner than a bee was.

The emptiness of the plains pressed in on him, and, for the first time, he felt a sliver of the fear he'd seen in June's eyes. One of being truly and utterly *alone.*

They rode west for hours, the sun climbing high and beating down on their necks. They spoke little, exchanging only a few practical words.

"Water?"

"Rider on the ridge yonder. Too far to make him out."

"It's just a deer."

Cole kept stealing glances at June.

She rode with a straight-backed competence that belied the terror he knew churned inside her. She scanned the landscape with a constant gaze, scouting ahead like a hawk.

He couldn't even imagine what kind of life she'd have had to lead to have honed her senses to a razor's edge like this.

How often did you go looking for trouble?

***

As evening bled purple and orange across the horizon, they found a place to make camp. A shallow hollow they could defend, one with a rocky outcrop protecting it on three sides.

Cole dismounted.

The physical exhaustion throbbed in his muscles, but it couldn't even begin to compare to the weariness all this silence was piling on his soul.

He gathered dry sagebrush for a small fire, while June rubbed the horses down with a practiced hand.

When the fire started crackling and casting a circle of warmth and light against the encroaching darkness, Cole and June sat on opposite sides of it, nursing tin cups of hot coffee.

"Ain't felt this spooked since I was a filly." June stared into the fire. "The night I lit out from that orphanage, felt like the dark was fixin' to swallow me whole."

"He ain't layin' a hand on you, June." He clenched his jaw. "I swear it on my own grave."

She turned her eyes to him. The way the auburn light danced on her face highlighted the contour of her jaw and cheekbones, her lips gleaming like rubies as she pursed them.

"I can't get a handle on you, Cole Slade." She tilted her head. "Ain't sayin' that's a bad thing. I just can't."

"What's there to get?"

"You're a good person. You're a capable worker. You could've had a great life in Oregon." She leaned forward. "I'm just a thief you should've turned in to the sheriff. Why give it up for me?"

He swirled the coffee in his cup. "Luke—the man who raised me—taught me that you stand for what's right. That you protect those who can't protect themselves."

She raised an eyebrow.

He chuckled. "I ain't saying you can't protect yourself. I just thought knowing right from wrong was a simple thing."

She shook her head. "Ain't that far from the truth?"

"Maybe the Cole Slade who rode out of Big Cedar wouldn't have helped you, but I've come to know you. You're all vinegar and fire, but there's kindness in you."

She looked down and smiled. "Thank you, Cole."

He took his bedroll and moved it from the far side of the fire, placing it a few feet from hers. As simple a gesture as it was, he hoped she would see it as he intended. Closing the distance between them.

"Get some shut-eye." He sat on his bedroll. "I'll take the first watch."

She watched him with an unreadable expression, then gave a small nod and turned her back to the fire, curling up under her blanket.

Cole settled himself with his back against a rock, his Henry rifle resting across his knees. He stared out into the star-dusted darkness, the weight of his promise settling onto his shoulders.

***

Clip-clopping snapped Cole awake.

The hypnotic crackle of the fire and the bone-deep exhaustion of the day must've lulled him to sleep. June was breathing evenly next to him. The sound, the shod hoof striking stone, was getting closer.

His every nerve singed.

He reached out and touched June's shoulder. She woke up in an instant with silent stillness, her hand already moving toward the knife at her belt.

"Riders," he whispered.

She crouched and rose to her feet with the fluid grace of a cat, sneaking to the edge of their hollow and peering into the darkness. Cole followed her a second later, holding his rifle at the ready.

Another sound drifted to them.

"...ain't see no fire..."

"Mercy." June's breath hitched. "And Griffin."

She hadn't mentioned them before, but Cole could tell those were the names of her former friends. Which meant that Jax had taken the bait. At least Cole didn't have to worry about the wagon train anymore.

Rushing back to kill the fire, Cole kicked dirt over it with his boots, smothering the flames until only a wisp of smoke remained.

June grabbed his arm. "This way."

"Where?"

"Dry wash, 'bout a quarter-mile north. Used to hide there as a kid. Spring floods cut a shelf under the bank. It's a tight squeeze, but it'll hide us and the horses."

"Won't he know to look there?"

"No." She winked at him." He was trying to sweet-talk me all the time. He was the one I was hiding from."

She untethered her horse, and Cole did the same. They led the horses by the reins, doing their best to make as little sound as possible.

The moon had ducked behind the clouds, plunging the world into disorienting blackness. June moved through it as if she had the eyes of an owl, her hand gripping Cole's arm.

He'd have to thank her for it. Ain't no way he'd have made the trip alone.

They found the cutbank, a dark slash in the earth. A narrow and claustrophobic space that a thousand years of water had carved out of the earth. It smelled of damp soil and cold stone.

They led the horses inside, their backs scraping against the low ceiling. Cole soothed them with a low murmur, pressing a hand over his mount's muzzle to keep it from whickering.

June pressed herself back against the far wall, and Cole stood beside her, his shoulder brushing against hers in the tight confines. They were close enough to feel the heat of each other's bodies and hear each other's ragged breaths.

Hoofbeats grew louder and closer. Saddle leather creaked. Voices murmured.

"...nothing. Told you he was sending us on a wild goose chase," a man said.

"Jax wants her found. So we find her," a woman said. "She can't have gotten far. Spread out. We'll check that ridge come sunrise."

The hoofbeats passed by Cole and June's hiding spot, so close Cole could feel the vibration in the ground.

He held his breath, every muscle in his body coiling as tight as a watch spring. June trembled beside him like plucked wire.

He put an arm around her, pulling her tight against his side. He didn't intend it as a gesture of romance; he wanted to shield and comfort her. To say *I'm here. You're not alone.*

She leaned into him, her head resting against his shoulder. They stood there, pressed together in the cold dark, as the sound of their hunters faded into the distance.

The immediate danger had passed, but Cole knew this was only the beginning. Until they could find a place to ambush the wolves, they'd have to scurry and hide. Worse, their attackers had the numbers and the ammunition.

Cole and June only had each other.

Chapter Twenty-Three

Early August 1852

Near Independence Rock and the Sweetwater River

June and Cole led the horses out into the open, the animals blinking in the new light with cool hides still warming after the night's chill.

The prairie unfolded in a wash of pale gold and soft greens under the sky, the color of faded blue fabric. Its beauty mocked June, showing her a pristine world that would go on being pretty even with the violence that stalked them.

Cole checked the loads on the horses.

He moved like a man who found comfort in performing tasks—in the predictable nature of tying a knot or checking a cinch. An ache June had never felt before unfurled in her chest as she watched him work.

He was so *steady*. A rock in the middle of the flood called 'her life'. He held fast and stood with her in the dark.

Cole glanced at her. "This country feel familiar?"

She exhaled.

He must've noticed her tear up as she scanned the horizon and the way her gaze lingered on a familiar dip in the land and a particular cluster of rocks. Of course, he had. They were riding east of the South Pass, toward the Sweetwater River. It had unlocked a door she had kept bolted for years.

This entire landscape threaded a tapestry of memories she'd tried to unravel and discard.

"More than I'd like." She gestured north, to a series of barren hills that shimmered in the distance. "The home I was raised in is over yonder. Just past them hills. Two days' ride, give or take."

Cole stopped what he was doing and turned to face her fully.

"The way you talk about Slade's Way makes it sound like something out of a storybook." Her tongue tasted of rust. "The St. Jude's Home for Unwanted Children had no Luke Slade. It was a workhouse with a chapel attached. We were free labor."

She looked down at her hands, remembering the constant hunger that gnawed at her belly and made a half-rotten apple she'd stolen taste like a feast. The lye soap that had scrubbed her skin raw. The cold that seeped up the floorboards and settled in her bones, one that made her shake to this day.

"How could anyone be that cruel to a child?"

"I don't think they did it on purpose. I reckon they were just worn down to the nub. Easier to see a mouth to feed and a back to break than a soul needin' comfort."

He clenched the saddle. "It was still cruel."

"It was." She lowered her head and smiled at him, unable to recall the last time anyone had cared enough to listen. "I can quiet up if this is troublin' you."

He shook his head.

"You learned. Learned not to cry, 'cause no one's comin'. Learned to fight for your crust of bread, or a bigger boy'd snatch it. Learned to be a ghost when you had to be, and as mean as a rattler when you couldn't."

She glanced at Cole.

The hand that had been tightening a strap now lay on the horse's flank. A muscle worked in his jaw, and he shifted his weight, turning his body more fully toward her. His eyes tracked from her face down to her hands, then back up, as if he were physically tracing the lines of her past onto the person standing in front of him.

"Trust was for fools," she said. "It got your boots stolen or earned you a beatin' for someone else's mischief. Kindness? That was a luxury we couldn't afford. That was my whole world. The only one I knew."

Cole frowned. "Until Jax."

June nodded. "He was older. Smarter. He saw the same things I did, but he saw a way out. He gathered us—me, Griffin, Mercy, Clay. A handful of us who were too tough or too stubborn to break."

He clenched hairs on the horse's side. "Straight to a life of crime."

She peeped at her fingers. "He promised us a world where we weren't just scraps off a rich man's plate. A world where we took what was ours. And for a long while... he wasn't wrong."

Old loyalty fought the bitter truth of what Jax had become. She *had* loved him once. It hadn't been in the way he'd wanted her to, but she had adored him with the clinging affection a sister had for the brother who'd pulled her from a burning building. He'd been her family, and he'd betrayed that trust.

"What about now?" Cole said. "What kind of life are you lookin' for, June? When this is all over."

Huh...

Good question. What kind of life was she looking for? She'd been so focused on running and surviving that she hadn't dared to dream of a *'when this is over'*. The future lay on a distant shore shrouded in fog. But, as she looked at Cole's honest face, a sliver of that fog began to burn away.

She chewed on her lip. "I don't rightly know. Not a traditional life, I don't reckon. I ain't the kind for a picket fence and a Sunday bonnet, I can tell you that. Too much mustang in my blood."

She looked out at the open country and endless sky.

"I want to be a partner. An equal. Pull my own weight, stand on my own ground... but not stand there by myself. You follow?"

He chuckled. "Someone to watch the back trail with?"

"Exactly!" She approached him and leaned on the horse. "To share a fire at the end of a long day."

As she spoke, the image taking shape in her mind cleared. She already had it. Right here, right now. She lived a life of adventure, riding in the wilderness alone with a man who treated her as his absolute equal.

A man she loved.

She looked away, certain he could see the truth written all over her face. "Someone to... to be happy with, I suppose. It's a foolish notion."

"It ain't foolish at all." Cole took a step toward her. "It's the only notion worth a damn."

She gulped. Her breathing quickened. Her chest pounded as she waited for him to close the distance between them and kiss her. Heck, if he didn't do it in the next five seconds, she was going to do it herself.

Then she made the mistake of looking to the right and caught the movement in the distance.

A dark mass of brown and white rippled in the distance, smudging against the plains as they grazed. There must've been thousands of them, the sea of shaggy hides and curved horns that could flatten Cole and June.

Behind the herd, the Thorns pointed their rifles up.

"Cole, we need to *move*," June breathed.

Cole's hand went to the pistol at his hip. "They wouldn't dare. They could be caught in it themselves."

"You don't know Jax!" She rushed to her horse. "He doesn't care! He'll burn down the whole world to get what he wants!"

As if to prove her words, the distant crack of rifle shots echoed across the plain. One, then two, then a volley. The peaceful sea of animals stirred. A ripple went through the herd, then a wave. A low rumble started, a vibration deep in the earth that grew from a murmur to a roar.

The herd turned and charged directly at Cole and June.

"Ride!" June jumped up on her horse. "Ride for the rocks!"

She pointed at a massive formation that rose from the plains a mile away—Independence Rock. They had no other hope of escaping the stampede coming their way. They leaped into their saddles and kicked the horses into a desperate gallop. The ground shook with the thunder of thousands of hooves pulsating through the earth.

The race flashed in a nightmare of dust and noise.

The air grew thick, choking them and filling their lungs with grit. The constant rumble and lowing drowned out every thought June had except *'faster'*. The herd flowed as a living avalanche behind them, a tide of dark bodies and flashing horns that was gaining on them with terrifying speed.

It happened in a heartbeat.

June's mare's front hoof caught in a rut. A sickening stumble, a high-pitched scream of pain and fear, and then the world was tilting and spinning. June flew for a fraction of a second before she hit the ground hard, the impact knocking the wind from her lungs.

Pain lanced through her shoulder, but it was nothing compared to the paralyzing terror that seized her. She rolled, gasping for breath, and looked up.

The stampede was a hundred yards away and closing.

She had no time. This was *it*. This was how she died. Trampled under a mountain of buffalo hooves.

"June!"

She looked up as Cole reined in his own frantic horse and turned around. That brave fool rode into the face of the charge to get her. His face was full of determination. June couldn't believe her own eyes.

He reached her and leaned down from his saddle. "Give me your hand!"

The herd had almost reached them. Fifty yards. The ground shook so violently she could barely stay on her knees. She scrambled forward, her legs refusing to work properly, and reached up.

His fingers closed around her wrist. "Hold on!"

He pulled her in front of him and spurred his horse. His arm wrapped around her waist like a steel band. They galloped the final distance to the rock, the hot breath of the lead buffalo on their heels. They reached the base of the massive granite dome just as the first wave of the stampede crashed around them.

Cole leaped from the horse, pulling her down with him. They scrambled up the sloping rock face, finding handholds, pulling themselves up just out of reach as the river of hide and horn flowed past, the bodies of the animals so close they could have reached out and touched them.

They collapsed onto a wide ledge as the herd thundered around the rock.

June glanced at Cole.

He had grime all over him, and his cheek was bleeding, but he was alive. They'd both made it through. Their mad dash had paid off.

She looked back toward the plains.

Cole's horse trembled at the base of the rock with its reins tangled but otherwise unharmed. Her mare was gone. Vanished. Likely dead under the stampede. Poor thing. She'd been June's companion for a *long* time, and June wouldn't even be able to say goodbye properly.

Jax.

That godless son of a gun had tried to kill her. There was no mistaking it. This wasn't a warning. This wasn't an attempt to scare her into coming back. He had unleashed an act of destruction on her. He'd been willing to see her die, to see them both die, trampled into nothing.

Guess I'm not his 'property' anymore.

June glared at the buffalo charging around them. She and Cole couldn't just *run* anymore. They couldn't look for the perfect ambush spot or make complicated plans. The time for debates and doubt had just ended. They couldn't afford to be prey anymore.

One way or another, they had to hunt the hunter.

Chapter Twenty-Four

Early August 1852

Near Independence Rock

The thunder of hooves faded, leaving behind a ringing void in Cole's ears that somehow boomed louder than the stampede had. The violent shaking of the earth settled. The cloud of dust that had choked them descended and revealed the world once more.

Pain shuddered in Cole's bones. His lungs burned, each breath rasping. He pushed himself up on trembling arms, scanning the scene below. His horse, thankfully, stood at the base of the rock. Of June's mare, there was no sign at all. The tide must've swallowed the poor beast.

He turned his head to June.

She knelt a few feet away with her back to him, staring out at the trampled plains. Her utter lack of movement reminded him of a statue. She'd come far from the girl who'd collapsed against him in the rain after the night riders and confessed her past in the gloom of the inn. Perhaps, she'd always been this strong. Maybe it'd just taken him this long to see it.

She could've died.

It burned his chest and knocked the wind clean out of him to think it, but it was the truth. If he'd been a second too slow, that stampede would've taken her. He'd never see her again. A part of him would've gone with her. The world would have become hollow and meaningless.

After all these years, his fear of abandonment, the ghost that had haunted his life at the orphanage as he watched brothers and sisters leave one by one, had finally found a face.

June's.

The thought of losing her brought him agony beyond reckoning. He'd left Slade's Way to find purpose and build something of his own. He realized now, with clarity that both blessed and cursed him, that what he'd been looking for had never been a place. He had found a person. And he would burn down the world to keep her safe.

He cleared his throat. "June?"

She turned her head slowly and narrowed her blue eyes. "He wanted us planted."

"Reckon so." He got to his feet and moved to her side. "Ain't about takin' you back. It's about puttin' you in the ground."

"Then it's high time we disappointed the man." She pushed herself up. "We gotta hit back."

Cole's mind whirred. He was the trail boss. It was his job to find a way out and make a plan. Running through the possibilities, he came across one dead-end after another.

Fight them head-on? Four against two, with them on horseback and him and June sharing a single mount. A fool's charge that would end with them both bleeding out in the dust.

Run? They'd last less than a day. Not only had the Thorns already tracked them successfully, sharing a horse would slow Cole and June to a crawl compared to the fresh mounts the Thorns had.

Hide? They had tried that. It had bought them a few hours, nothing more. Jax would methodically sweep the entire territory until he found them.

Every scenario he chewed up spat out the same conclusion.

"We have to set a trap," Cole said. "Find a place where their numbers don't matter."

June's gaze swept past the rolling plains and the distant river and settled on a jagged line of hills to the northeast.

She frowned. "I know the place."

Cole waited.

"The Blackwood Prospect," she said. "An old silver mine. Went bust 'bout twenty years back. Company lit out in the dead of night, left the whole works to rot. Just a ghost town now. A boneyard full of bad luck."

Another part of her childhood, then.

"Matrons at the home used to spin yarns about it. Said it was haunted. Ghosts of greedy prospectors snatchin' up wicked children, draggin' 'em down the shafts. 'Course, some of the older boys snuck out there. Called it a deathtrap. Nothin' but caved-in tunnels, rotten wood, and pits that dropped straight to perdition."

Cole nodded. "You think we can use it against Jax."

She turned to face him. "He's all pride, that one. Big and empty as this sky. Us walkin' away from that stampede? He'll take that *personal*. He'll figure we're spooked, runnin' scared and witless."

"What's to stop 'em from chargin' in, all four at once?"

She snorted. "He'll want the last dance for himself. Wants to be the one to corner me, to look me in the eye when it's done."

Cole looked from her determined face to the distant hills. In any other circumstance, he'd call it a long shot at best, and a

196

desperate gamble doomed to fail at worst. He did trust June, however. He had faith in her intellect and her knowledge of Jax's mind. If she said it would work, it would.

"Alright," he said. "Let's go see about this ghost town."

***

The climb down from Independence Rock took a while longer than the climb up.

With no stampeding buffalo threatening to trample them, and Cole's muscles long having cooled off from the adrenaline of the chase, he could hardly move. He imagined it was the same for June.

By the time they reached his horse, and he soothed it enough for it to let them mount it, the sun was beginning its descent, painting the sky in strokes of orange and blood red.

He swung into the saddle, then reached down, his hand closing around June's.

She sat in front of him, pressing her back into his chest. Her warmth seeped through his thin shirt, and the steady rhythm of her breathing filled his ears.

They rode to the Blackwood Prospect as twilight bled across the land, the horse moving with a steady gait. The landscape grew harsher, the gentle plains giving way to broken country littered with rock and scrub. The hills loomed larger, their peaks jutting out like broken teeth against the darkening sky.

An hour later, they saw it.

A collection of skeletal buildings huddling in a narrow valley formed the mining town. The headframes of the mines stood like gallows against the last of the light. Heaps of gray tailings rose like ancient burial mounds. A wind moaned through the gaps in the dilapidated buildings, mourning with the sound of people who'd died steeped in failure and forgotten dreams.

Cole reined in the horse at the edge of the settlement, and they slid to the ground.

"We need to be smart about this," he whispered. "We need to find the right spot. A place that's defensible, where we can make our stand."

June scanned the collection of ruined buildings, her eyes moving from the collapsed smithy to the row of miners' shacks, to the brooding structure that must have been the main office. Her gaze went off into the distance, as if she was seeing the scary stories of her childhood overlaying the image of the place as it had once been.

Then her eyes locked on a small building set a little apart from the main cluster. An assay office, where they'd have weighed and tested the ore. The unassuming little hut had a sagging porch and a single door hanging askew on its hinges.

She pointed at it. "There."

Cole frowned. "It's too small. No cover. We'd be trapped like rats."

"Not in it." She smirked. "Under it."

She led him to the building. The assay office was in better shape than most of the other structures, but the floorboards of the porch groaned ominously under their weight.

"One of the boys from the home, he took a shine to me. Spun a yarn to try and impress. He and his friend, they dared each other into this office one night. His friend went first. Took one step inside and... poof. Gone. Boy said he heard a scream, then dead quiet."

She pushed the door open, revealing a dust-choked room. In the center of the room, a section of the floor had collapsed, revealing a gaping hole.

"Found the friend a week later. Bottom of an old air shaft. Company dug it to vent a main tunnel, then just boarded it over for this office. Wood's all rotted through by now. It's a straight drop. Thirty feet, maybe more."

Cole peered into the darkness of the shaft. It reeked of damp and dead air rising from the ventilation tunnels that fed into it. He picked up a loose stone and tossed it in. He waited. One second. Two. Three. Then, a faint, distant *thump* echoed up from below.

He looked at June. "You certain he ain't wise to it?"

"Boys rarely liked me *and* Mercy. It's a safe bet that she doesn't know."

"It's a gamble, but I trust you." He nodded. "You think he'll take the bait?"

She giggled. "You asked that already."

He sighed. "I'm just worried. I can't understand how he could be that stupid."

"He always was when it came to me."

Well, assuming Jax behaved as June said, it was a perfect trap. It used Jax's own arrogance and obsession against him. It negated the strength of his gang, turning the confrontation into a one-on-one contest on ground of their own choosing.

"We'll need to make it look right," Cole circled the opening. "We can't just leave a gaping hole in the floor. He's not a fool. He'll see it."

"We cover it," June looked around the room. "We make it look like the floor is solid."

***

They got to work.

Cole found a rusty pry bar in the ruins of the nearby blacksmith's shop. With it, he pried up the floorboards around the edges of the hole, weakening their supports, making them fragile and unstable. He worked with focused intensity, the sound of splintering wood echoing in the dead silence of the town.

June, meanwhile, gathered debris. She found rotten canvas, scraps of old tar paper, and handfuls of the thick dust that covered everything.

They laid the supports back loosely over the chasm, then carefully placed the weakened floorboards on top, creating a treacherous false floor. It was a flimsy illusion, but it would, hopefully, hold long enough.

Finally, June scattered the canvas and dust over their work, artfully arranging it to look as if years of neglect had created the scene instead of minutes of desperate labor. When they finished, the floor looked solid, if a little uneven. It appeared *untouched*.

A trap ready to be sprung.

They stood back, surveying their handiwork in the fading light.

"I'll need a place to hide," Cole said. "Close enough to see, close enough to act if... if this doesn't work."

June pointed to a cluster of collapsed barrels just outside the office's single grimy window. "There. You'll have a clear line of sight."

He nodded. The plan was set. Every piece was in place. All that was left was waiting.

He looked at June. Her face was pale in the gloom, but her eyes were bright and clear. She was no longer running. She was standing her ground, ready to face the monster she had helped create.

June took his hand and led him outside. "When he comes, you must be the one to run."

"Why?"

"That's what he'll believe. What he'll *want* to believe." She sighed. "Seeing someone like you flee like a coward will make him feel less small."

Cole interlaced his fingers with hers. "Alright. But you better be careful."

She smiled. "I will."

He squeezed her hand and strolled with her through the alleys of the dead city, waiting for Jax to show up.

Chapter Twenty-Five

Early August 1852

Blackwood Prospect

Jax moved through the skeletal remains of the Blackwood Prospect like a king patrolling his rightful domain. The wind mourned through the gaps in the rotted timbers of the headframes, whispering stories of broken dreams and greed turned to dust.

This had grown on the promise of riches and fell to the inevitable rot of time. It reflected Jax's philosophy perfectly. You either took what you wanted, or the world took it from you and left your bones to bleach in the sun.

He'd left the others circling the perimeter.

Griffin's face had been a mask of thinly veiled terror, and his arguments against this course of action had finally dried up Jax's patience. Luckily for Griffin, the coward had fallen in line after two slaps.

Clay—a man whose loyalty was as blunt and uncomplicated as the butt of his pistol—had simply nodded.

Mercy had been the most unsettling. She'd watched him with those dark eyes of hers, and he couldn't figure out the emotion behind them for the life of him. Satisfaction? Resentment? She'd always been jealous of June, of the place she held in Jax's mind, and he knew a part of her would be glad to see this whole bloody affair finished, one way or another.

"There are army scouts thick as fleas on a stray dog in these hills," he'd told them. "You three ride the rim of this valley. Keep your eyes peeled. If you see bluecoats, you fire one shot and ride like hell. I'll handle this myself. I don't want a full-scale war party drawn down on us before I've collected my due."

He'd lied, of course.

Oh, the soldiers undoubtedly buzzed around somewhere close like flies, but he had another reason for sending those three away. He was shedding his pack. This last act had nothing to do with the whole gang.

This moment belonged to him and him alone.

Well, him and June. He'd sever the last festering tie to weakness he could no longer abide. Put down the orphan boy who'd dared to stand in Jax's light and touch Jax's property. That kind of reckoning needed privacy. He wanted to savor the look in their eyes as he dismantled their pathetic little world.

Stalking through the shadows of collapsed buildings, Jax tasted the air, reading the story of the place in the disturbed dust and the single set of fresh tracks leading deeper into the town. Rounding the corner of what had once been a livery stable, he came upon his prey.

They stood in the open, near a small building that looked like it might collapse if a strong wind blew on it.

They *held hands.*

The sight of it set Jax's nerves on fire. A gesture of comfort or alliance, Jax could handle. He'd kill them and be completely calm. *This* shouted romance at Jax, and he would punish it severely. He'd make it slow. Crush that orphan's hand, which had dared lace its fingers with June's.

Jax stepped out from the shadows, clenching his Colt in his hand.

"Well now," he said. "Ain't this a touchin' picture."

They turned like one, their clasped hands breaking apart. Slade pushed June behind him, using his body as a shield. Brave, but useless. A mess of bruises and dried blood littered the boy's face, and his nose had swollen and bent, but his eyes held a steady and unwavering fire.

He's not afraid. The fool is actually not afraid.

June looked at him differently, too. The terror he had seen in her before had vanished and given way to the hard and cold stare he'd always known. The face of the girl he had trained. The fighter. For a fleeting second, a sliver of pride pierced his rage. *He* had taught her that.

"It's over, Jax," she said.

"Over?" He let out a soft chuckle. "Darlin', it's only just gettin' to the good part."

Cole glared at him. "Leave her alone."

Jax leveled the barrel of the Colt at Cole's heart. "You back away from her, boy. This is family business. Don't concern the likes of you."

"I reckon it does concern me," Cole put his hand on the handle of his own pistol. "She's with me."

"She is *mine*. I found her in the dirt, I put food in her belly, I made her what she is. She's property I'm reclaimin'. And you... you're just somethin' that got in the way." Jax clenched his hand. " Now I'm sayin' it plain. Step aside."

"No," Cole said.

Jax frowned.

He'd already resigned to killing June the moment he'd unleashed that stampede on her. But, even with that in mind, it hurt to see what had happened to her. How much she'd changed. This *boy* had poisoned her. At this point, killing her would be doing her a favor. It would cleanse her of the stain.

Of course, the boy had to die first, and June had to watch. Jax had to make her understand the futility of her choices. Then he would deal with her.

He fired.

The shot cracked through the dead silence of the town. But Slade dived to the side, pulling June with him. The bullet chewed a chunk of wood from the corner of the building behind them. Slade then came up firing. Jax ducked behind the corner of the livery, the shot whining past his ear.

The fool can shoot.

The fight descended into a deadly dance among the ruins. Shots echoed, ricocheting off rotted wood and stone foundations. Dust kicked up from the street, mingling with the acrid smoke of gunpowder.

Jax, of course, was the better shot. More practiced. More ruthless. He moved with liquid ease, using the crumbling structures for cover, his mind working through angles and opportunities to inflict pain and injury.

He clipped Slade's shoulder, which made the boy grunt in pain and stumble, a flash of red blooming on his shirt. Victory was coming. Jax had the boy pinned down behind a stack of rotting barrels.

"You see, June?" his voice brimmed with triumphant malice. "This is what happens when you put your faith in sheep! They just know how to bleed!"

Jax broke cover, sprinting across the open ground to get a better angle and finish this once and for all. To hell with dragging it out. Putting a bullet into that son of a gun's face would have to be satisfaction enough.

Slade looked at June and then did exactly what Jax had expected from someone like him.

The boy ran, scrambling away toward the derelict assay office.

A guttural laugh tore from Jax's throat. A sound of pure, ecstatic vindication. He had been right all along. All their talk of honor, of standing ground, of goodness—it was all a lie. When faced with real violence, the self-righteous always broke. Their pretty codes of conduct shattered like cheap glass. They were cowards at their core.

"That's it, boy! Run!" Jax laughed and shot into the air. "Show her what you're really made of!"

This was *perfect*. Even better than Jax could've planned. He could hunt the boy down like the terrified rabbit he was, and June would be forced to watch. She would see the pathetic collapse of her newfound ideals.

The thrill of the chase and the absolute certainty of his own superiority consumed Jax as he ran. His fingers slick with sweat and clumsy with adrenaline, he fumbled to reload. Pulling the leather pouch of cartridges from his belt, he tried to thumb fresh rounds into the cylinder while keeping his eyes locked on Slade's fleeing figure of Slade.

In his haste, his grip slipped. The pouch tumbled from his hand, spilling its precious contents into the thick dust of the street.

"Damn it!"

He kept going. One shot remained in the Colt, and that was all Jax needed. One bullet would put a hole in the back of a running coward's head just as well as more.

Jax closed the distance.

Slade scrambled through the open doorway of the assay office and disappeared inside. Jax nipped at his heels with a triumphant grin on his face. He burst through the door, his eyes adjusting to the dim interior, raising his pistol for the kill.

Slade cowered in the far corner. Jax smirked and strolled forward, savoring the sweet, sweet—

The floor gave way.

One moment, Jax stood on solid ground. The next, wood splintered with a sharp *crack* that melted into Jax's own strangled cry as a horrifying void appeared beneath his feet.

He fell.

The drop sickened him as he plunged into a pool of suffocating air and darkness. His arms flailed, reaching for a foothold and failing to find any. His stomach leaped into his throat. A fleeting square of gray light—the hole in the floor— receded above him with impossible speed.

Impact.

He smashed into the ground with a bone-shattering crash. An explosion of white-hot pain blasted in his left leg with a grinding *crunch* that sent a wave of nausea through him. He landed in a heap of rock and splintered timber at the bottom of the shaft, the Colt flying from his grasp.

He lay there, gasping.

The thick and stale air smelled of damp earth and a century of decay. He tried to move, to push himself up, but another bolt of agony shot from his leg, so intense it made him cry out. He looked down. His leg was twisted at an obscene angle below the knee.

He was trapped.

Panic began to coil in his gut like a serpent finding a fresh hunting ground for the first time. He pushed it down with a surge of fury. He was Jax Rae. He did *not* panic. He was the wolf, not the rabbit in the snare.

He scrabbled around in the darkness, his hands searching for his pistol. His fingers closed around the familiar cold steel. He had his gun. He could still fight. He would wait. They would come to gloat, to look down at him, and he would—

He thumbed the hammer back and checked the cylinder.

Empty. How?

The shot in the air...

The one he'd fired out of sheer joy that his prey was running. He'd spent it and never even realized it. The rest of his ammunition lay scattered in the dust thirty feet above him.

His gun was useless. He was helpless.

A shadow fell over the square of light from above. Two figures appeared. Slade and June leaned over the edge of the hole and gawked down at him.

He wished they'd gloat. But their expressions held only final judgment.

Slade tilted his head. "It's over, Jax."

Jax snarled, trying to push himself up, but the pain in his leg anchored him to the grimy ground. "This changes nothing! You can't keep me here!"

"We don't have to," June said. "The army will be here by mornin'."

She stepped back from the edge, her silhouette disappearing. Slade gave him one last look, one that held not a shred of pity, then he too left.

Jax remained alone in the dark.

Water *drip-drip-dripped* somewhere in the tunnels, and his own breath sawed in and out of his lungs. Had he fallen better, he might've been able to crawl through one of the tunnels leading into the shaft and try to escape.

Instead, he could only wait here.

He could only stare up at the small square of sky. A prisoner in a tomb of his own making. A king with a broken crown in a kingdom of dirt and darkness. For the first time since he was a terrified boy his parents abandoned, Jax Rae felt helpless.

Chapter Twenty-Six

Mid-August 1852

Returning to Fort Laramie

Cole and June rode between two groups of plodding horses.

In the front, a grim sergeant led twelve uniformed soldiers, whose blue coats slashed a jarring slit of order against the untamed land. In the rear came the prisoners.

Jax lay strapped to a litter slung between two pack mules. His leg, crudely splinted by the army surgeon who had accompanied the patrol, jutted out at a stark angle. His face, pale beneath a layer of grime, remained a mask of defiance.

Every jolt of the litter resulted in a new groan. Yet, even broken and bound, he had a venomous energy coiling around him. The palpable aura of a cornered rattler whose back had broken but whose fangs retained their poison.

Cole would be glad to see him go.

Behind Jax rode the rest of The Thorns, their wrists cuffed, their expressions a study in defeat.

Clay, the brute, sat slumped in his saddle, his heavy-lidded eyes fixed on the rump of the horse in front of him. Griffin's face bore soul-deep weariness, and he looked almost serene, like a man someone had finally freed from a lifetime of carrying a crushing weight. Mercy rode last with a ramrod straight posture, staring ahead with barely a blink.

June rode beside Cole.

She sat tall on her horse, holding the reins loosely in one hand. The fugitive she had been had vanished. The fire of the last few days had scoured the haunted girl who'd flinched at shadows. In her place sat a woman who had faced her own personal devil and stared him down into a pit of his own making.

Cole's own body throbbed with a symphony of aches.

His shoulder pulsed with a dull beat where Jax's bullet had grazed him. His nose made every breath a conscious effort. A deep fatigue had settled into his bones, one that went far beyond tired muscles.

He had faced down a killer, felt the primal urge to kill in return, and walked away the victor. But victory felt less like a trumpet blast and more like the hollow echo after the canons had shot their canon bolts for the final time.

Luke Slade's lessons on right and wrong seemed like quaint theories from a distant and simpler world. He had learned the hard truth out here. Justice required more than a strong moral compass. It required a steady hand, a willingness to stand in the path of a storm, and the grit to look pure evil in the eye and refuse to blink.

The sergeant, a grizzled veteran named Cutler with a thick mustache and eyes that had seen too many miles, dropped back to ride alongside him.

"That's a fine piece of work, son," Cutler said. "A damn fine piece. We'd have been chasin' those devils clean to the Rockies if you hadn't got the drop on 'em."

Cole shrugged. "Thank you."

Cutler grunted and glanced back at the prisoners. "Right sizable bounty on that one's head. Enough to stake a man proper. Figure it'll be split between you and the girl. Fair's fair. You earned every cent."

Cole thought of the worn leather pouch with its meager collection of coins he'd carried from Big Cedar a lifetime ago. The bounty meant security and a stake in the future, but all he could think about was the cost. A broken man on a litter, a woman, and two men looking at a future behind bars, and the ghosts of the men they had killed.

Granted, the Thorns *had* done awful things, and Cole would step up to protect innocents from people like that ten out of ten times. He simply lamented their poor choices. As June had said, not everyone had a Luke Slade.

He looked at June.

As if feeling his gaze, she turned her head to meet his eyes. A question hung in the space between them. What now? They'd bound in chains the shared threat that had forged their unlikely alliance, that had burned away her secrets and his naivety.

With the danger gone, what was left?

He had fought to keep her safe, and now that she was, she was also *free*. Free to ride away. Seek that future she'd spoken of, one that might have no place in it for a rough-edged boy from an orphanage who was still figuring out how to be a man.

His old fear, the one he thought he'd outrun, came galloping back. He had found his purpose, his partner, his home, all in the heart of this one fierce, complicated woman. And now he stood to lose it all.

***

As Fort Laramie appeared on the horizon, a smudge of adobe and wood against the immense blue canvas of the sky, a knot tightened in Cole's chest. They'd stepped out of the wilderness, but he felt more lost than he ever had in his life.

A roar of sound and motion welcomed them.

Men poured out of the sutler's store and the blacksmith's shop, their faces alight with curiosity that quickly turned to joy. Women appeared in doorways, wiping their hands on their aprons, their expressions a mix of relief and awe. Children, who had been playing in the dusty street, stopped their games and stared with wide eyes.

"They got 'em! By God, they got The Thorns!"

Men he'd never seen before slapped him on the back.

"Good on you, son!"

"You showed 'em what for!"

Travers pushed his way through the crowd, his good arm waving for them to make way. His injured arm was still in a thick sling, but the color had returned to his face, and his eyes were sharp and clear.

He stopped in front of Cole's horse, looking up at him, and the look on the old trail master's face was worth more than any bounty. One of profound, unwavering respect.

"Slade," Travers said. "You magnificent, foolhardy son of a gun. You actually did it."

Cole glanced at June. "We did it."

Travers' gaze shifted to her, and his expression softened.

"That you did, lad. That you did." He looked back at Cole. "I knew you had sand. I didn't know you had a mountain of it. Luke Slade would be proud of the man you've become."

Cole smiled.

He'd left Slade's Way to prove himself and step out from Luke's long shadow. He hadn't wanted the responsibilities of leading that orphanage. Yet, he'd led a wagon train west and brought a notorious gang to justice.

As much as he'd tried to run from it, being a leader had found him. The only difference was that, now, he'd learned to accept it with grace.

Cole and June said goodbye to Travers and rode out of Fort Laramie just as Sergeant Cutler and his men herded the prisoners toward the sheriff's office, which also served as the fort's jail. The crowd followed in a shifting mass of boisterous bodies. Cole had never seen so many people so eager to see a gang locked away.

He led her to a quiet spot near the riverbank, where willows grew thick, and only the gentle sound of water echoed. Where the setting sun cast auburn shadows across the ground, and the light gleamed off the murmuring water like bits of gold.

Right there, next to the waterside, Cole and June slid from their horses.

He needed to get this talk with June out of the way sooner rather than later. Whatever her choice ended up being, he needed to know so he could get on with his life one way or the other.

Their whole history flashed before his eyes as he looked at her face. The meeting. The charade engagement. The public lie. The secrets, arguments, and attacks. The stampede. Everything that had led to this one moment.

He stared into her eyes. She started back.

Okay... how do I start this?

214

Of all the things Luke had prepared him for, this wasn't among them. What was he supposed to open with? *'I love you'*? No, that'd be too strong. It'd ruin any chances of this working. He had to ease her into it. Yeah, that was it. Start with something more chewable and then get to what he needed to say.

"June..." He cleared his throat and looked down. "It's over. You're safe now. Truly safe."

She smiled. "Yeah."

"The bounty is a lot of money," he gulped. "It's enough for a clean start. Anywhere you want to go. Oregon, California, back east, if you've a mind to. You're free. You don't owe anyone anything. Not the law, not the train. Certainly not me."

"I know."

"What I mean is, well, you don't have to stay with me." He rubbed the back of his head. "I mean, you don't have a reason to, so—"

"Cole," she giggled. "Are you tryin' to say somethin', or just kickin' up dust?"

He took a deep breath. Here it came. Now or never.

"Yes." He exhaled. "I love you, June. And I'm askin' you to stay. With me. Or I'll go with you. Whichever way the trail leads, long as we're on it together."

June took a step closer to him, closing the small distance he had so carefully put between them. She reached up, her fingers light as a feather, and gently traced the line of his bruised and broken nose.

"You are the biggest fool I ever met, Cole Slade," she whispered.

"Right... I figured as much. A woman like you—"

"My whole life, I've done nothin' but run. From the law, from men like Jax... from my own shadow. Runnin's all I've ever known." She took a shallow breath. "I'm tired of runnin' away, Cole. I'm done with it."

She moved her hand from his face to his chest, her palm resting flat over his heart.

"Being out here... with you... it's the only time I ever felt I was runnin' to somethin'." A small smile touched her lips, a fragile thing that made Cole's heart ache. "Feels like every wrong turn I ever took was just leadin' me down the path to you."

The dam inside him broke. Every fear, every doubt, every bit of the hard-won control he had maintained washed away in a powerful flood. He cupped her face in his hands, his thumbs stroking the high curve of her cheekbones.

She was real. She was here. She was choosing to stay.

"June," he said. "I need you to be very clear right now."

She laughed. "I love you, Cole Slade. Is that clear enough?"

He pressed his forehead against hers and nodded.

"I could never leave you," she whispered, her voice breaking. "Don't you know that? I think my life only started the day I met you."

He lowered his head, and she rose on her toes to meet him.

Their lips met, and the world fell away. It was a kiss of quiet homecoming. It tasted of dust and sunlight and the hard-earned promise of a new beginning. A silent vow and a partnership sealed with truth revealed in the quiet twilight.

When they finally broke apart, they kept their foreheads together, their breath mingling in the cool evening air. The roar of the celebrating crowd from the fort was a distant, meaningless sound from another world. The only world that mattered was right here, in the circle of their arms.

They had faced the storm and found their harbor in each other.

Chapter Twenty-Seven

Late August 1852

Fort Laramie

A week passed.

The fort became a place of healing for June. The physical wounds had begun to mend. The cut on her head had scabbed over, the deep bruises mottling her body had faded from angry purple to sickly yellow-green.

The deeper wounds, the ones on her soul, took longer to heal.

They hurt less like open gashes and more like bones that ached with the memory of the break. The fear still lingered like a phantom limb that tingled in the dead of night, but June had been learning how to hope.

This morning, that hope stretched particularly thin. Today was the day of the trial.

The drab dress of her flight, the symbol of her ruse as a helpless woman, lay folded and forgotten in a corner. She wore the sturdy canvas britches and work shirt she had chosen for herself. Those fitted her like a second skin.

A firm knock sounded at the door.

"June?" Cole said. "It's time."

She took a deep breath, straightened her shoulders, and opened the door.

He stood in the hallway, his large frame seeming to fill the narrow space. He had shaved that morning, a small act of civility both touching and absurd, given what they were about to face. He'd combed his dark hair back from his face, and he wore a clean shirt—one of the two spares he possessed.

He offered her a small smile that failed to reach his eyes. "You ready for this?"

June's palms grew slick. "Ready as I'll ever be."

He held out his hand. "Let's go."

She placed her hand in his. His calloused fingers closed around hers. The contact sent a current of strength through her, chasing away some of the cold that had settled in her core.

Together. A novel concept, one she was still learning the shape of.

They walked out of the inn and into the bright sunlight of the fort's main street. People stopped what they were doing to watch them pass. Settlers, soldiers, trappers who had heard the story—all eyes followed Cole and June.

She could hardly believe it.

A week ago, she'd been an object of suspicion. The strange girl who'd brought trouble. Now, she was one half of the duo who'd brought down the Thorns. The shift in perception was dizzying, a cloak of a different color that felt just as ill-fitting as the last.

The trial took place in the fort's mess hall.

The long room had a low ceiling and smelled of stale coffee, packed bodies, and sawdust. The fort's commander, Major Harris—a man with a hawkish face and a chest full of medals— presided as judge, his presence lending a grim military authority to the proceedings. A jury of twelve had hastily

219

assembled—six soldiers and six sober-faced settlers, men who looked more accustomed to holding a plow or a hammer than deciding the fate of another man.

Cole led June to two chairs near the front. They sat with their hands still clasped together between them. The murmuring of the crowd died down as the heavy door at the back of the hall creaked open.

They brought Jax in first.

He lay on the same litter, carried by two burly soldiers. They'd put his shattered leg in a brace and cleaned him up. Still, a washed face and combed hair did nothing to soften his feral behavior.

He scanned the room, his gaze dismissing the judge, the jury, the entire assembly, until it landed on June. He met her eyes, and a cold smirk twisted his lips. A look of pure hatred. A promise of retribution that transcended chains and prison walls.

One that said, *'This isn't over. It will never be over.'*

June squeezed Cole's hand, and his grip tightened in response. She lifted her chin and held Jax's gaze. She'd put him in that pit, and she would never look away from him.

Clay came next, flanked by two more soldiers. The big man looked lost, like a powerful dog whose master had been struck down. Griffin looked like a man who had been expecting this day for a long time and had finally reached the end of a long and painful road. He took his seat and stared at the rough-hewn table in front of him.

Last came Mercy.

She walked with a venomous grace. Her dark eyes found June's and locked onto hers; the look in them chilled June more than Jax's outright hatred. It was a look of acid jealousy, a lifetime's worth of resentment honed to a razor's edge. The face of a woman who had lost everything and blamed the girl who sat holding another man's hand.

Major Harris banged his gavel. "This court is now in session."

The proceedings began with a dry recitation of charges read out by a young lieutenant acting as prosecutor. Robbery, assault, murder. When the time came, the lieutenant called his first witness.

"The prosecution calls June Crow to the stand."

June's heart leaped into her throat. This was it. The final, irrevocable act of betrayal. The ultimate severing of the twisted family ties that had bound her for years. She let go of Cole's hand and stood, her legs wobbling like hollow reeds. She walked to the witness stand and swore the oath on a worn Bible.

"Miss Crow," the lieutenant said. "Please tell the court about your association with the accused."

Her voice trembled on the first few words. "We grew up together. At St. Jude's."

She drew a deep breath and told the story. A chronicle of their descent. She spoke of the early days, the petty thefts born of hunger and desperation. She painted a picture of a band of lost children clinging to each other for survival, led by a charismatic boy who promised them a better life.

Then, her voice hardening, she spoke of the change.

She told them about Benton County, the deputy who had tried to stop them, whom Jax shot down for the simple crime of doing his job.

221

"He changed," she said, looking directly at Jax. "Or maybe he just showed his true colors. The taking wasn't about survival anymore. It became a sport. He started to enjoy the fear. He liked the power it gave him."

She described the attack on the Pony Express rider. The cruel, pointless game of it. She recounted the events leading up to the stampede, her voice cracking as she described the moment she realized Jax was willing to kill her, to see her trampled into the dirt rather than let her be free.

"He told me I was his." She glared at him. "His property. Something he owned. But I am not a thing. I am a person. And I chose to walk away from a man who believes strength is measured by the suffering of others."

The lieutenant nodded slowly.

"Thank you, Miss Crow." He turned to the judge. "The prosecution would now like to call Cole Slade."

Cole took the stand. He recounted the attacks on the train, detailing Jax's infiltration, the confrontation at Fort Laramie, and the final trap at the Blackwood Prospect. He spoke with a simple, unadorned honesty that held more power than any fiery rhetoric.

When he finished his formal testimony, he paused and looked directly at the jury. "Sirs, I know what some of you might be thinking. You look at Miss Crow, and you see her connection to these men. You might wonder about her part in it."

June's heart clenched.

What is he doing?

"I want to tell you what I see." Cole's dark eyes swept over the jury and landed on June with a look of fierce loyalty. "I see a woman who found the grit to turn her back on the only family she ever had when they turned to killin'. A woman who, with her own life on the line, cooked up a plan to lead a pack of wolves away from good folk. Who stood her ground in that dead town and saw justice done. She's the reason the Thorns ain't a plague on this territory no more. She's my partner. And she's the gutsiest soul I've ever had the honor to know."

A hot sting pricked the back of June's eyes.

He hadn't needed to do this. Her agreement with the sheriff had guaranteed her immunity for revealing the location of the Thorns' loot. But no immunity deal would ever affect the court of public opinion.

What Cole had just done, taking her messy story and holding it up to the light as a testament to her strength, would do more for people's opinion of her than anything she could've ever said.

The rest of the trial was a formality.

The jury deliberated for less than an hour before they filed back in. The foreman—the blacksmith—stood and read the verdict in a booming voice that left no room for doubt.

"Guilty."

One by one, on every charge.

Major Harris delivered the sentences without ceremony. For Clay, Griffin, and Mercy, long years of hard labor at the federal prison in Leavenworth. Jax, the only one to have murdered anyone, would be going to the hangman.

The soldiers dragged him from the room.

It was over.

***

Cole and June walked out of the mess hall and into the afternoon sun, blinking like creatures emerging from a dark cave. The world seemed brighter, the air cleaner. It was the first breath of a new life.

Travers waited for them with a proud grin on his face, clapping Cole on his good shoulder.

"Knew you had the sand for it, son. The both of you." He looked from Cole to June. "You two make one hell of a team."

June smiled. "Thanks, Boss."

Travers nodded at her. "Well, now that mess is swept and settled, we ought to palaver about what's next."

She blinked. "What do you have in mind?"

He looked at Cole. "First train's already headed for Oregon, but there'll be others, soon as this wing of mine is mended. I'll be needin' a top hand, Slade. The job's yours if you'll take it."

June's smile turned softer.

It was everything Cole had set out for. A purpose, a position of respect, a future earned with his own two hands. June's heart stuttered, a painful mix of pride for him and a renewed fear of being left behind. His adventure was just beginning. Where did she fit into that?

Cole looked at Boone, then he looked at June.

"I'll take the job, Boone," he said. "On one condition."

Boone raised an eyebrow. "And what's that?"

Cole reached out and took June's hand, lacing his fingers through hers in a gesture that was no longer a lie or a charade. "You take us both."

Boone threw back his head and let out a great laugh that echoed across the fort. "I wouldn't dream of separating you two. I'm curious, though, is it to be another fake engagement?"

June blushed and looked away. "No... It's a real one this time."

Boone's eyes widened. "You sure as hell don't waste time, do you, son?"

Cole shrugged. "What can I say? Can't risk her changing her mind."

Boone laughed again. "Aint' that the truth? C'mon, then. Drinks are on me!"

Epilogue

Summer 1857

Heading to Wind River Range

Five years later, the trail held a different song.

It hummed in the leather of Cole's saddle, in the whisper of the high-altitude wind through the lodgepole pines, and in the steady rhythm of two horses climbing toward the roof of the world.

The Oregon Trail Cole had travelled half a decade ago—that flat, dusty, sprawling beast of the plains—had given way to this grand and rugged scripture of stone. The jagged peaks of the Wind River Range clawed at the deep blue sky, their granite faces catching the last of the afternoon sun and blazing with a cold light.

The air scoured a man's lungs with the clean scent of pine and cold rock and the promise of winter.

This land tolerated human presence but offered no warm welcome. It demanded respect, resilience, and a quiet sort of courage. Cole breathed it in and felt, for the first time in a long time, a profound and settled peace.

He had come home to a place he'd never been before.

He reined in his horse, a sturdy buckskin gelding, and waited for June to draw alongside him. She rode a spirited dapple-gray mare, handling the animal with an unconscious grace that was a part of her now.

The five years had been kind to her.

They had sanded away the defensive edges and left behind a relaxed trail hand. Lines of laughter had begun to form at the corners of her eyes, faint etchings that told a story of shared jokes and quiet contentment.

She pulled up beside him. "Taking in the view, trail boss?"

"Just figuring a spot to make camp. Yonder, I reckon." He pointed with his chin toward a sheltered meadow, a patch of impossible green nestled in a crook of the mountain between a stand of aspen and a fast-moving creek. "Good water, good grazing, and a solid rock face at our back. Can't ask for better."

"You learned a thing or two from Boone Travers," she said.

He shrugged. "A man pays attention. Or he ends up bein' food for the buzzards."

They rode down into the meadow, the silence between them filled with the unspoken language of a long partnership. They moved with practiced efficiency, two halves of one whole.

Cole slid from his saddle and began unsaddling the horses, his large hands moving with a sureness he hadn't possessed five years ago. June, without a word, began gathering fallen wood for a fire.

As he rubbed down the buckskin, his thoughts drifted back to the boy who had undertaken that first journey.

That eighteen-year-old Cole Slade felt like a stranger now, a younger brother he remembered with a kind of fond pity. A boy bursting with Luke's noble ideals but utterly unprepared for the world's harsh realities. A boy who thought adventure meant a lonely ride into the sunset, who mistook his fear of being left for a desire to be alone. He had wanted to find his purpose out here in the wild west, and he had. He just never imagined his purpose would have a name, and that name would be June.

The news of Luke's passing had reached them two years ago in a letter that had taken six months to find them in a small trading post on the Green River. He had died peacefully in his sleep, one of the older orphans had written. Slade's Way was in good hands, now being run by a man Luke had trained himself.

Cole had read the letter by a flickering fire, the familiar grief of loss a sharp, clean ache in his chest. He had mourned the man who had been his only father, whose code he had carried with him like a talisman.

He had wept, and June had held him, her quiet strength a bulwark against his sorrow, saying nothing, but simply being there. That night, looking up at a sky full of stars so bright they seemed to hurt, Cole had made a silent promise to the memory of the man who had raised him.

He would build something good in this wild land. Something that would last. Something of which Luke would have been proud.

Their trading post.

It had been their shared dream for three years now, a plan they'd honed over countless campfires and whispered in the dark of their bedrolls. A place of refuge and supply, nestled here in the Wind Rivers—a final stop for weary travelers before the last hard push into Oregon country.

The very place of fair trade, honest dealings, and a warm fire Cole and June had lacked so many times crossing the Trail with Travers. A beacon of the very decency Luke had championed.

June had the fire going now, a cheerful crackle of flame that pushed back the encroaching evening chill. The scent of coffee soon mingled with the sharp scent of pine. She handed him a tin cup, her fingers brushing his, a small, familiar touch that sent a jolt of warmth through him.

She settled on a log across the fire from him. "You're quiet tonight."

He took a sip of the scalding coffee. "Just thinkin'. About Luke."

She nodded, her expression softening. "He'd have loved this country. The sheer size of it."

"He would have. He'd have probably tried to name all the mountains and write a book of poetry about 'em." A sad smile touched his lips. "I wish he could've met you. I think he would've seen right away what I took so long to figure out."

"And what's that?" she said with a playful glint in her eye.

"That you're the stubbornest, most difficult, and finest woman this side of the Missouri."

"Only this side of the Missouri?" She put her hand on her chest. "Oh, the betrayal."

He laughed. "Sorry, sorry. Will 'in the world' do?"

She pouted. "Perhaps…"

After that, they ate in a comfortable silence, the easy quiet of two people who no longer needed to fill every moment with words. The last of the sun's light vanished from the highest peaks, and the sky deepened to a velvety, ink-black dome studded with a billion diamonds.

As they watched the celestial display, a single star streaked across the sky, a fleeting silver tear.

"Make a wish," June whispered.

Cole watched the quiet ache he knew all too well flash over her face in the firelight. The one sadness in their otherwise joyful life. The one dream that had remained stubbornly out of reach.

For all their partnership, all they had built together leading trains back and forth along the trail, the one thing they had not been able to create was a child of their own.

The army surgeon at Fort Bridger had been kind but blunt. The hard years of June's youth, the malnourishment of the orphanage, the brutal toll of life on the run—had all left their mark. The chances of June ever conceiving a child weren't zero, but they might as well have been.

It was a quiet grief they rarely spoke of, but it lived in the spaces between them.

Cole felt it as his own failure, a bitter pill he could never quite swallow. He could face down outlaws and lead families through the wilderness, but he couldn't give this magnificent woman the one thing he knew she wanted the most.

He saw the way her eyes lingered on the children in the wagon trains they led, the soft, wistful look on her face as she watched a mother soothe a crying baby.

It was a knife twist in his gut every single time.

He reached across the fire and took her hand. "What did you wish for?"

She looked down at their joined hands, her thumb stroking the back of his. "The same thing I always wish for."

"I know. I'm sorry."

She looked up, her eyes watering. "I just... I see the families we bring west. I see the love they have, the way they look at their children, and I think... I just wish we could have that."

"June—"

She squeezed his hand. "I've been thinkin'. About us. About the kind of life we want to build here. We talk about the trading post, about creating a place of safety and fairness. Maybe... maybe it's meant to be more than that."

"What do you mean?"

"What if we find others like us, Cole?" she said. "The ones left behind and alone."

He looked down. "There are orphanages along this trail, June."

"Yeah, and I'd wager most of 'em are more like my St. Jude's than your Slade's Way. Places where children are just mouths to feed, with no one to stand for them, no one to show them what's right."

She leaned forward, her eyes blazing with a fire that took his breath away.

"You had a Luke Slade, Cole. A man who gave you a name and a code and a home. He showed you that you were worth something. What if... what if some boy or girl out there, some lost soul shivering in the dark, just needs a Cole and a June?"

The suggestion pulled at his heartstrings.

So simple, perfect, and profoundly right that it reframed his entire purpose on this trail. It answered a question he hadn't even known to ask. It closed a circle and weaved together every thread of their lives—his blessed past, her broken one, and their shared hope for a better future.

He stared at her.

The idea bloomed in his chest with joy so potent it stole his breath. Adopt. Create their own family through choice. Give back and help those who were like them. It was the most beautiful, most logical idea he had ever heard.

"We could do it," she pressed on, her face alight with the passion of her conviction. "We could build our trading post, and we could build a family. We could give children a home. A real one. A place where they know they are loved, where they are safe."

He got up from his log, walked around the fire, and knelt in front of her. He took her face in both of his hands.

"Yes," he said. "God, yes."

Tears finally spilled from her eyes. He wiped them away with his thumbs.

"We'll do it," he said, his own eyes burning. "We'll find our family."

He thought of the trading post, their shared dream. It had always been for them, a place to put down roots. Now, it would be for others too. It would be a legacy.

"What should we call it?"

"How about... Slade's Way West?" He smiled. "In his honor and ours."

June's smile through her tears was the most beautiful sunrise he had ever seen.

She threw her arms around his neck, pulling him into a fierce hug, and he held her tight, burying his face in her hair.

They clung to each other by the light of the fire, under a vast canopy of stars, as a family at the very beginning of their greatest adventure.

Made in the USA
Monee, IL
30 October 2025